www.HarperLin.com

Americanos, Apple Pies, and Art Thieves

A Cape Bay Café Mystery Book 5

Harper Lin

ISBN-13: 978-1987859430
ISBN-10: 198785943X

Contents

Chapter One

I watched as Sammy's face contorted into a grimace, her lips stretching into an exaggerated frown and her eyes squinching up like she was trying not to cry. She stuck out her tongue and smacked her lips a couple of times.

"No," she said, shaking her head vigorously as she put down the cookie in her hand.

"That bad?"

She took a big gulp of water from her bottle and swished it around before swallowing it and answering me. "Yes."

I picked up another one of the cookies from the plate. "Really? When I tried them,

I didn't think–" I paused to take a bite then grabbed a napkin to spit the dry crumbs out.

Sammy handed me my water.

It took a couple of swish-and-swallows, but I managed to get the awful taste out of my mouth. "They did not taste like that when I tried them fresh out of the oven."

"I would hope not."

"Okay, so, no on the spicy pumpkin flaxseed branola cookies." I dumped the plate into the trash on top of the not-quite-as-awful pumpkin-filled spice scones. At least those hadn't felt like I was eating sand.

"With a name like that, did you really think they sounded good?"

I shrugged. "They sounded healthy."

"So no."

"They weren't bad when they were still warm."

"But they weren't good either." Sammy's big blue eyes looked at me, daring me to say that the cookies had tasted great hot.

"They didn't taste like I was licking dirt."

"Close enough. What's next?"

We were in the back room of Antonia's Italian Café, the coffee shop in Cape Bay, Massachusetts, that my family had owned for three generations now. Sammy and I had cleared the desk of everything that usually covered it (the computer, several stacks of paper, two boxes of napkins, a vacuum-sealed bag of Sumatran coffee beans, and one suspiciously furry-looking cupcake wrapper of unknown age), spread out an assortment of fall—and pumpkin—themed potential menu items, and embarked on a taste test that so far had ended up with decidedly mixed results.

Along with the spicy pumpkin flaxseed branola cookies and the pumpkin-filled spice scones, the cinnamon cupcakes with pumpkin filling and the pumpkin shortbread cookies had been failures. They, at least, had avoided the trash can.

Sammy and I had declared them edible but not menu-worthy and set them aside to be taken home to our eat-anything boyfriends. Well, to my eat-anything boyfriend and to Sammy's eat-anything nonboyfriend. She still wouldn't admit that she and Ryan were dating, even though they spent almost every evening together and made googly eyes at each other every time they were in the same room.

We'd had a few successes in our testing too, fortunately. Sammy ate her whole slice of pumpkin bread and then went back for another. The apple-cinnamon muffins made with locally grown apples and fair-trade cinnamon were to die for. And the pumpkin spice panettone was utterly mouthwatering. All we had to do now was settle on the recipe for the all-important pumpkin spice latte.

Compared to the rest of the world, we were behind in adding pumpkin-spice-everything to our menu for the fall. It was my first year running the café, and it hadn't even crossed my mind until Sammy brought it up a few days after I'd gotten home from my Italian vacation.

She'd been digging through one of the boxes in our latest supply shipment when she looked at me sitting over at the desk doing the books.

"When's the pumpkin spice syrup coming in?" she'd asked. "I thought for sure it would have come in while you were gone, but it hasn't yet. It's not backordered, is it?"

I froze at the computer and hoped Sammy wouldn't notice that I hadn't answered her.

No such luck. "Fran?"

"Um."

"You *did* order the pumpkin spice syrup, didn't you, Fran?"

I turned around slowly. "Um... I forgot?"

"Oh, my gosh, you're joking, right?" Her big blue eyes looked at me desperately.

"Um..."

She collapsed half into the box. "You're kidding me. You forgot the pumpkin spice syrup? People have been asking for pumpkin spice lattes for weeks now, and I just keep telling them it will be here any day!"

"Why didn't you tell me?" I asked, my voice getting a little high.

"I thought you knew!" Her voice got even higher.

"I had no idea!"

"Have you placed our next order yet? Can you add the pumpkin spice syrup on there?"

"I placed it yesterday afternoon. It's already shipped."

"You're killing me, Fran. Killing me!"

That conversation had led directly to our taste test. Sammy reminded me that we typically added not just pumpkin spice lattes to our menu but also an assortment of fall-themed baked goods. I ordered the pumpkin spice syrup and spent several hours online looking up the recipes we'd just taste-tested as well as a few more that had been rejected before they made it out of my kitchen.

Now there was just one thing left to sample.

"I actually have a couple of different pumpkin spice latte recipes for us to try," I said tentatively. I hadn't told her that I was looking at different recipes, but when I came across the first one online, I felt like I had to give it a chance. And one of the recipes was unbelievably delicious. But I needed Sammy's opinion.

"Really?" she asked.

I nodded quickly. "Let me run out front and make them, and then you can try them."

"Okay."

I hopped up out of my chair, grabbed a container from the refrigerator, and hurried out front to make the drinks. A few minutes later, I was back in the storage room, drinks in hand. I put them all down on the table in front of Sammy.

"Which one should I try first?" she asked, looking at each of the three cups in turn.

"This one." I pointed to the one on the far left.

She picked it up and sipped it. "Tastes like a pumpkin spice latte."

I nodded. It was made with our usual recipe—pumpkin spice syrup bought from our distributor and mixed into a latte—so her reaction was what I expected.

"Next one?"

I nodded again.

Sammy tasted it. "Ooh, that's good!" She took another sip. "What's different?"

"I made the syrup myself."

"It's tasty. I like it." She looked suspiciously at the third cup without letting go of the second. "What's different about that one?"

"Try it."

She gave me a skeptical look. "Is this the weird one? The spicy branola latte? Or the punkinnamon cappuccino?"

"Punkinnamon?" I asked.

"Punkinnamon," she repeated. "Like branola. Except pumpkin and cinnamon."

"Oh!" I laughed. "Is that a thing, or did you just make it up?"

"Just made it up." She smiled her patented brilliant Sammy smile at me. "It sounds real though, doesn't it?"

"Yeah, actually." I laughed again.

Sammy took another sip from the second cup. She didn't look interested in trying number three.

"So, are you going to try the last one?" I asked.

She wrinkled her nose. "Do I have to?"

"Well, you don't *have* to..." I let my voice trail off suggestively.

"But?" she asked, squinting in my direction.

"But if you don't try it, I might have to put it on the menu anyway and tell everybody that it's Sammy's secret recipe."

Now she glared. "Okay, I'll try it." She put down the second cup. "But is it weird? Should I be prepared to rinse my mouth out?" She glanced around the table for her water bottle. "I don't want that branola lingering longer than it has to."

"It's not weird," I said. "It's just another pumpkin spice recipe. And I don't think you could mix branola into a drink anyway. It's too... gritty."

Sammy made a face and moved her mouth like she was reliving the unpleasant taste of the failed cookies.

"Just try it. I promise it's not awful—"

Sammy picked up the third cup and brought it to her lips.

"—I hope." I said it late enough that she already had the cup tipped back and the coffee spilling into her mouth. I had tasted the drink right before I brought it to her, so I knew it was good. In my opinion anyway. There was always a chance that Sammy could completely disagree.

For a second, I was afraid she was going to spit the latte at me, just reflexively at my suggestion that I wasn't one hundred percent sure of its deliciousness. Fortunately, she didn't. Instead, her eyes got even wider than usual. She swallowed and immediately took another sip.

"That's amazing," she said after swallowing.

I couldn't help but break into a grin. The third one was the one I'd put real effort into−probably more than I really should have. But once I got started tweaking the recipe, I couldn't stop myself until it was perfect. And it was perfect.

"What−?" Sammy started.

"Completely from scratch," I said, anticipating her question. "And with real pumpkin."

"Seriously? It has pumpkin in it?" She took another sip.

I nodded. I was beaming. "Most of the time, a pumpkin spice latte is just the spices you use in pumpkin pie. Well, it's that or syrup flavored like that. But I found this recipe that called for actual pumpkin. And then I found one for the pumpkin pie spice blend. So I realized I could just make it completely from scratch. You just mix the spices and toast them a little and then add the pumpkin and−" I realized I was chattering and probably going into far more detail than Sammy needed or wanted. "And I may have gotten a little carried away."

"You should get carried away more often. This is really great." She swallowed down some more.

"So, do you think people would mind if we switched over to this?"

"Are you kidding?" she asked, emptying the cup. I'd only filled it partway, but still—she'd taken it down in record time. "I think people would mind if they found out we kept serving them the regular stuff when we could have been giving them this."

I could barely contain myself, I was so excited. I'd spent so much time tweaking the spice blend and getting the proportions just right that I would have been incredibly disappointed if she didn't like it or if she thought it wasn't any better than the syrup we bought. The feeling more than made up for the cookies that hadn't tasted good.

"So when can we start selling this stuff?"

I surveyed the table. There wasn't enough there to sell—it would be gone as soon as we put it out.

"Tomorrow?" she asked hopefully.

I cringed. Sammy's giggle told me that my reaction didn't surprise her.

"Let me guess," she said. "It's not that you can't cook it all tonight, it's that you don't want to have to have it here first thing in the morning."

She wasn't wrong. It would take a few hours of hard work in the kitchen, but I could have plenty of each new menu item ready for the morning. Staying up late enough to prepare everything wasn't the problem. Getting up in time to bring it in was. I was not a morning person. Especially not café-early morning. I could stay up half the night without trying, but being at the café when it opened was painful, especially this time of year when the sun didn't come up until well after we'd opened. I let Sammy be in charge of opening up each day, and I handled closing. "You know me too well."

"You're just a little predictable sometimes is all."

As much as I would have enjoyed lingering and just chatting with Sammy, I knew we had to get back to work. "I should have enough of the pumpkin spice mix to get us through the day if you want to go ahead and switch to that one," I said, standing up from the table.

"Yes!"

I had to laugh at her enthusiasm. I was glad that she liked the new recipe so much though. "Okay, well, let's get this stuff cleaned up, and I can show you and the girls how to make it."

"Hey, do you want to take the leftovers and give them out as free samples of the new menu items?"

"That's a really good idea. Create demand from our customers. I like it."

I hadn't made much of each recipe, so we worked on cutting up the muffins, bread, and panettone into bite-sized pieces, stabbed them with toothpicks, then arranged them onto plates. I carried them out into the front of the café and explained what they were to Becky and Amanda while Sammy worked on getting the desk set back up

"Have you ever heard of an artist named Cliffton? Louie or Lewis? L-O-U-I-S," Sammy asked when I came back into the stock room.

"It's Louie. The French pronunciation. Why?"

"Just curious." She arranged some papers in a stack and put them on the desk. "Is he famous?"

I thought for a moment. "Yeah, pretty famous. I mean, he's art-world famous. Not like Monet or Picasso or anybody like that, but some of his work's in the Museum of Modern Art back in New York. They probably have some at the Institute of Contemporary Art up in Boston too. I think one of his pieces went for a couple million at one of the auction houses last year."

"Wow. He's a painter?"

"Mm-hmm." I fiddled with the placement of the computer monitor on the desk.

"What kind of painter?"

I looked up at Sammy curiously. "Why are you so interested in Louis Cliffton?"

She shrugged. "I just heard his name and was wondering about him. What kind of art he does and all. I figured you would know." She went back to moving things around on the desk.

I stared at her. There was something she wasn't telling me. I knew she was a pretty good artist, but I didn't think it was anything she'd considered seriously. I tried to think of what I knew about Cliffton, but I couldn't come up with much. My old public relations firm back in New York had been in the running to represent him a few years earlier. I'd had his résumé memorized at the time, but now I couldn't even remember where he'd gone to school. "He's an abstract expressionist."

"That's like Jackson Pollock, right?"

"Yes." I watched Sammy's face in case it gave anything away. Maybe Sammy was thinking about going to art school? I didn't think abstract expressionism was her style, but maybe he was doing a residency at a school she was looking at.

"Why are you looking at me like that?" she asked.

"I was just trying to figure out why you're so interested in him."

"So interested?" She laughed. "I just asked a couple of questions!"

I thought for a second about whether I should really say the next thing I wanted to. Ultimately, it wouldn't hurt anything if I was wrong, and if I was right, at least it would be out in the open. "Sammy, are you thinking about going to art school?"

"What?" She laughed again. "No! Why would you think that?"

"I don't know. I guess it just seemed weird that you would pull Cliffton's name out of nowhere and ask me about him."

"Well, I didn't exactly pull it out of nowhere. He's having a show in Cape Bay."

Chapter Two

"What?" I was sure I hadn't heard her right. Louis Cliffton? Here? In Cape Bay? It made no sense. He rarely even did shows in New York and LA. Why on earth would he have one in sleepy Cape Bay? "Are you sure?"

"Yup," Sammy replied.

"Louis Cliffton?" I enunciated his name. Maybe she had actually said someone else's name and I just misheard her.

"Yes, Louis Cliffton."

"Here?"

"Yes."

"In Cape Bay?"

"Yes." Sammy kept her voice exceptionally calm and rational. "The artist Louis Cliffton is having a show here in Cape Bay." She paused. "Massachusetts. Where we live."

"Where?"

Sammy looked at me like she wasn't quite sure if I was all there. "Here. In Cape Bay. Where we live."

I realized I wasn't being clear. "No, I mean, where in Cape Bay?" It wasn't exactly like we had art galleries lining the streets. More like kitschy souvenir shops, and most of those were closed for the season.

"Oh, down at the museum."

Of course. The Cape Bay Museum of Art. The Shuster family had opened it up back around when my grandparents opened Antonia's. They exhibited work from artists around New England but with a preference for Massachusetts and the Cape Bay area. I remembered going there with my mom when I was a kid. She'd take me around and talk to me about the paintings, pointing out the themes and the artists' techniques. It was where I'd learned to love art.

I'd stopped in only once since I came back to town. It wasn't the place I remembered.

It wasn't just that it seemed smaller than it had when I was a little girl. It was also run-down. There were weeds growing up through cracks in the parking lot and trash littering its edges. Inside, the floor tiles were clearly aging, and the furniture that dotted the space was worn threadbare. The dropped ceiling had more than a few water spots.

All that I could have excused if it weren't for the art on the walls, or rather, the lack of it. Some of the pieces that had been Mr. and Mrs. Shuster's prizes were gone, replaced with paintings that weren't much better than what I could do, and I hadn't taken an art class since middle school. There were several paintings by artists not from New England, which I could have forgiven if I wasn't pretty sure at least one was a replica of one of the glorified paint-by-number canvases some friends of mine in New York had painted at one of the home art parties that had gotten trendy over the past few years. I wasn't sure if it was better or worse when I came across a gallery of the museum dedicated to the local elementary school's art class projects.

"Why on earth is Cliffton having a show here?" I asked, more to myself than to Sammy.

"Beats me," she said with a shrug. "All I know is they're having some big party to celebrate the opening on Friday night."

"What? They are? Is it open to everyone, or is it invitation only?" I was suddenly very excited as the news of the show began to sink in. There were plenty of pictures of Cliffton's works online, but I'd only ever seen one or two in a museum, and not a little museum like ours either. Only the kind of massive museum that's all marble. Never an exhibition. And now there was going to be one in Cape Bay? Where I could drop by on my way to work in the morning just to take a peek? I still didn't understand it, but I didn't need to understand it to be excited.

"Invitation only," Sammy said. I'd almost forgotten that I'd asked her the question.

"Do you know how to get an invitation? Do you have one?" A museum exhibition opening would be such a fun date with Matt! We could get dressed up, go to the opening, go out to dinner, go back to his place or maybe mine...

"I think they sent them to prominent people in town. The mayor, of course, the town council, the chief of police. I know Mrs. D'Angelo got one since she's the head of the Ladies' Auxiliary—"

Of *course* Mrs. D'Angelo had one. She was the town busybody. She was everywhere all the time, in a whirlwind of words and heavy floral perfume.

"—a lot of business owners."

"Wait, business owners?"

Sammy nodded.

"I'm a business owner. Why didn't I get one? Everyone loves Antonia's! The mayor's in here every day! Is it because I only just came back to town?" My feelings were a little hurt. Just because I'd only recently moved back into town after being gone for fifteen years didn't mean I wasn't just as much a part of the community as anyone else. Antonia's had been a Cape Bay institution for almost seventy years!

"No, I don't think how long you've been in town has anything to do with it." She fiddled with something on the table.

"Then why didn't I get invited?" I realized I was probably overreacting, but that's the thing with overreacting—you can't exactly stop yourself.

"But Fran—"

"Does someone have a grudge against me?"

"Fran—"

"It's not because the pumpkin spice stuff was late getting on the menu, was it? I mean, that seems like a silly reason not to invite me to a big event like this."

"Fran!"

"What?"

Sammy's mouth twitched. "You did get invited. Your invitation's right here." She picked up the thing she'd been fiddling with and handed it to me.

It was a gorgeous cream envelope made of what was obviously expensive paper. My name was embossed on the front in an elegant script.

Ms. Francesca Amaro and Guest

It was still sealed. I grabbed the letter opener from the desk and slid it under the flap. The invitation itself was just as gorgeous and elegant as the envelope.

You are cordially invited to an
Exhibition Opening
at
The Cape Bay Museum of Art

Featuring
Glimmer and Glare
the new series by
Louis Cliffton

Wine and Hors d'Oeuvres will be served

"How did you know what was in the envelope?" I asked. "Did you get invited too?"

"Me?" Sammy scoffed. "No. I saw Mary Ellen's invitation when I was over at the gift shop yesterday."

"Oh, okay." I ran my fingers over the embossed words. I felt bad that Sammy hadn't been invited. As much as I thought it would be a perfect date for Matt and me, Sammy would probably appreciate the art more. "Do you want to be my plus one?"

"You don't want to take Matt?"

"No, I do! I just figured that you'd probably enjoy it more than him, and since you didn't get invited..." I trailed off. I'd known Sammy casually for years when she was working at the café, but we'd never really gotten close until I'd moved back to town to take over the café after my mother died. I didn't have many friends in town anymore—most of them had moved away after high school—so I was excited about my fledgling friendship with Sammy. Still, I wondered if it would seem weird to her that I was offering to take her to the opening over my boyfriend.

"Oh, no, Fran! Take Matt! It'll be a fun date for you two! You can get dressed up, go to the opening, get some dinner, maybe take a romantic walk on the beach." She sighed. "The show's going to be in town for two weeks. I have plenty of time to go."

"But have you ever been to a museum exhibition opening? They're fun."

"No, I haven't, but, honestly, I'd rather wait and go look at the art when the museum's more peaceful and not filled with people who are more interested in free food than fine art."

I stared at her for a second. "For someone who's never been to an exhibition opening, you seem to have a pretty good idea of what they're like."

Sammy laughed. "Well, I've overheard a lot of conversations in this café over the years, and I can't think of a single one that was about any kind of art other than a kid's school project. I've also served a lot of people, and I've seen their reaction when you give them a free sample. They're definitely more enthusiastic about those." She paused. "Speaking of free samples, should we go see how the samples we put out are doing?"

"You really think there will be any left? I've seen our customers' reaction to free samples too."

Sammy laughed. "Well, we should at least go out there so you can show me and the girls how to make the new pumpkin spice latte."

"Maybe we can even give out a few free samples!"

Sammy and I went out to the front—we were right, the samples were all long gone—and I showed her and the girls how to make the new version of the latte. It wasn't hard—I did all the heavy lifting making the mix—they just had to learn the right amount to use and remember to mix it into the milk before steaming instead of adding it after, like we did with the syrup. I made the first two and gave them to Becky and Amanda to taste.

"This is supergood!" Becky said, her curly red ponytail bobbing at the back of her head.

Amanda nodded vigorously before taking another long swig from her cup.

Then I had each of them practice making one. And then, since the café wasn't very busy, we each made another one and gave them out as free full-size "samples" to customers who had been watching us practice. Predictably, they were thrilled.

We had just finished up when Matt walked into the café.

"*Ciao, bella!*" He walked right up to me and kissed me.

I blushed. "Matty!" I said quietly. It wasn't so much that I disliked public displays of affection as that they felt awkward when we were in my place of business in front of my employees and my customers.

"*Scusa, Francesca,*" he apologized. He had picked up a handful of Italian words on our trip and now used them at every possible opportunity. It was sweet and silly.

"You're out of work early." I silently dared him to reply in just Italian.

"*Sì*," he replied, calling my bluff.

I rolled my eyes and tried to think of a more open-ended question to ask him. "So did you just come to see me or were you thirsty?"

I could tell I caught him. His warm brown eyes narrowed as he thought.

"The answer is always that you just came to see Fran, Matt," Sammy offered.

I gave her a dirty look. "The point was to make Matt say it in Italian."

"Oops!"

"*Sempre tu*," Matt said to me. Always you. He turned to Sammy. "*Grazie, Samanta*."

"*Prego*," she replied.

"What? Since when do you speak Italian?" Sure, it had only been *you're welcome*, but still! I didn't know Sammy knew a single word of Italian beyond, well, cappuccino, latte, tiramisu, espresso, and a few more words that were kind of necessary to work in the café.

"I worked here back when your grandparents were alive, Fran. I didn't pick up much Italian, but I will never forget that whenever someone thanked your grandfather, he always said *prego*."

I stood dumbfounded for a second. I had forgotten that. As soon as she said it, I could picture him again, standing behind the counter, smiling, and saying *prego* every time someone said thank you.

"I forgot about that." I smiled, remembering it. And then Matt cleared his throat, bringing me back to the present. "What?" I asked innocently. "Did you need something? I thought you just came to see me."

He grinned. "*Un caffè americano si prega.*"

I rolled my eyes again. I had walked right into it. I sighed. "Becky, could you make an americano for Matt?"

Becky stood there for a second, staring.

"An espresso with extra water," Sammy whispered.

Becky's face scrunched up. "Isn't that basically just regular coffee?"

I sighed and rubbed my forehead.

"It's *fancy* regular coffee," Matt said.

"It's a completely different brewing method," I muttered. At least she got him to speak English.

"Here, I'll show you how to make it," Sammy said, going over to help Becky.

"I'm going to have to give them remedial coffee lessons." I kept my voice down. Becky was a great employee the vast majority of the time, but every once in a while, I wondered if she paid any attention at all. This was one of those times.

"Aw, give her a break. She's young," Matt said, putting his arm around me.

"When I was her age, I was roasting all the beans for the café."

"That's because you have coffee in your veins instead of blood." He tipped his head close to my ear. "That's why you're so hot and strong-bodied."

"Matty!" I elbowed him in the side.

He yelped and jumped away, but he was grinning.

"Here, Matt, try this." Sammy held a cup across the counter towards Matt.

"If it's bad, do I get a replacement for free?"

"If you think it's bad, I'll dig one of Fran's spicy pumpkin flaxseed branola cookies out of the trash so you can taste something that's actually bad."

"Hey!" I exclaimed.

"They weren't good? I told you they wouldn't be," Matt said.

"You didn't even try one!"

"I didn't have to. You told me the name."

Sammy burst out laughing.

"I can't get a break with the two of you," I said.

Before either of them could pile on me more, the bell over the door jingled and Sammy's not-boyfriend Ryan walked in.

"Hey, Fran! Matt!" He paused for a second then said, "Hi, Sammy," like she wasn't the first person his eyes landed on as soon as he walked through the door.

"Oh, hi, Ryan." Sammy stood there nonchalantly, acting like she didn't care that he had just walked in, even though she was practically glowing. "Can I get you anything?"

He leaned on the counter in what I thought was an attempt to look casual, but that only succeeded in making him look like an awkward teenage boy trying to look cool around his crush.

"I could go for something. Is anything particularly good today?" Ryan, even more obviously than Matt with me, had really just come in to see Sammy.

"We have a new recipe for the pumpkin spice latte. It's pretty amazing." Sammy was practically cooing.

"That sounds great! I'll have one of those!" he said, a little too enthusiastically. While Sammy started making his drink, he turned to me. "Hey, thanks for inviting us over for Thanksgiving!"

"Oh, you're welcome. The more the merrier!" I said that, and I kept inviting people like I meant it, but the more people I invited, the more anxious I got about it. It had started on a whim—Matt and I were both newly alone in the world, and I thought it would be nice to invite a few friends over for Thanksgiving instead of it just being the two of us. "A few friends" had turned into more than a few, and now I was pretty sure half the town was coming. I was starting to get a little panicky about it.

"I really appreciate it. My family's just up in Plymouth, but since I'm the rookie, I have to work the holiday, so I'm not going to be able to make it up there. I was looking at a Thanksgiving dinner from McDonald's until Sammy said you invited us."

I seriously doubted Sammy would have let him have Thanksgiving dinner at McDonald's. She might disguise it as making sure all the Cape Bay Police Department officers working that day had a real Thanksgiving dinner, but she wasn't going to let Ryan eat fast food on the holiday. I wasn't going to say that though.

"Let us know if we can bring anything. Sammy's a great cook, and I can buy a mean package of dinner rolls."

"I'll let you know once I figure out what I'm making."

"Great!" He looked up at Sammy, who was walking around the counter with his latte.

"Do you want me to bring this over to your table for you?" she asked.

"That'd be great!" Of course he didn't mind. And of course he wouldn't mind if she sat down for a minute to chat. And of course he wouldn't mind sitting there making googly eyes at her for the next twenty minutes or so. They really were adorable together. I didn't know why they denied they were together, but that didn't make them any less adorable.

"Hey!" I blurted, turning to Matt. I had suddenly remembered the Cliffton show. "We don't have any plans Friday night, do we?"

"That depends."

"On what?"

"Whether you arranged for us to have dinner with the New England Patriots or you want me to go clothes shopping."

"What if I want you to go clothes shopping with the New England Patriots?"

"I'd do that." I was pretty sure he'd do almost anything if it involved the Patriots.

"Actually, there's going to be this art show in town—"

The door to the café flung open again, and before I could even think that the afternoon rush must be starting, the whirlwind was flying at me.

"Francesca!" Mrs. D'Angelo called out, much louder than our proximity required. "Francesca, have you heard the news?"

"What news, Mrs. D—"

"There's going to be an important show at the Cape Bay Museum of Art! Featuring the works of the great Louis Cliffton! Can you believe it? Cliffton!" She clutched my arm with her long red fingernails.

"Yes, I—"

"His paintings go for millions, Francesca. *Millions*! And he's doing a show here! In Cape Bay! Do you know why?"

"No, actually—"

"His mother grew up here! So he's decided to have his newest collection debut at our little museum! I'm just beside myself! His grandmother was the chairwoman of the Ladies' Auxiliary! Long before my time, of course, but I feel such a connection knowing we have that in common. You got your invitation to the opening?"

"Yes—"

"Of course you did! And you're coming, of course! Bring darling Matteo here with you!" She reached out the hand that wasn't attached to my arm and dug it into Matt's shoulder. "I'm so happy for the two of you, by the way. Finding love with each other when you both had no one else in the world. So touching! You did get together quickly after Carmella and Gino died, but grief does funny things to people. I'm not one to judge. Anyway, I just wanted to stop in to make sure you'd received your invitation! I have to be off! Lots of work to be done before the opening! See you Friday!"

And she was gone. Everyone in the cafe sat in stunned silence as it tried to recover from the barrage of words and the cloud of perfume.

"Wow," I thought I heard Ryan say.

Matt rubbed his shoulder. "So I guess that's the art show you were talking about?"

"Yup, that's the one."

"He's some big-deal artist?"

"Internationally known."

"Sounds fun."

"Yup."

I looked at the indentations in my upper arm where Mrs. D'Angelo's fingernails had been. At least now I knew why Cliffton was having his show in Cape Bay.

Chapter Three

A few days later, Matt was sprawled on my couch watching ESPN with two lattes—one was my mutt-looking purebred Berger Picard, named Latte for his fur that was exactly the color of a perfectly made latte, and the other was a pumpkin spice latte I'd brought home with me for Matt.

He had developed a bit of an addiction to them in the couple of days they'd been on the menu. I was getting a little worried about what he would do when we weren't selling them anymore. Probably beg me to make them for him at home.

I was upstairs in the little room that had been mine since my childhood, when I'd lived in the house with my mother and grandparents. Despite planning for months now to move into my grandparents' old room—the master—downstairs, I hadn't done it yet. It still needed a fresh coat of paint and new furniture, and lately I'd been thinking about replacing the carpet downstairs, probably with hardwood. I wasn't sure if it was sentimentality holding me back from getting it all done or something else, but I was still sleeping upstairs.

I was halfway dressed for the gallery opening. I had my dress and shoes picked out and lying on the bed, and my hair was dry. I wrapped a section of it around my curling iron.

My hair was black, mostly through the grace of genetics and partly through the help of Clairol. I normally didn't bother with curling it since it was naturally wavy and also because it was so thick that it seemed to take a lifetime to curl it. Tonight was a special occasion though, and I was going all out. I didn't get many opportunities to get all dolled up, so I was taking this one and running with it.

"Are you almost ready?" Matt called from downstairs.

"Almost!" I called back, even though I had a feeling my definition of "almost" wasn't the same as his. I checked the clock on my phone. I had plenty of time before we had to leave, especially since we were driving over instead of walking like we usually did when we went anywhere in Cape Bay. We were going out for a nice dinner in the next town after the opening, so the car was a necessity.

I finished curling my hair and started on my makeup. I decided to play up my eyes and go with a natural-looking pink-color lipstick since I planned to enjoy my dinner, not worry about messing up my lipstick. A little bit of golden-brown eyeshadow and liner and my eyes looked brighter and bluer than I thought they ever had. I topped them off with mascara then slipped into my dress and the highest heels I owned.

I checked myself out in the mirror. I couldn't help but think I looked pretty good. I was excited to see what Matt thought. I grabbed my little clutch, slid my phone in, and headed for the steps. In my mind, I was picturing those scenes in movies where the girl comes down the stairs all decked out and her boyfriend is waiting at the bottom, suitably amazed by her appearance. It wasn't really like that, of course.

For one thing, Matt wasn't waiting for me at the bottom of the stairs. I kicked myself a little for not yelling down to him that I was ready. Besides that, you couldn't even see the stairs from the living room where Matt was stationed. Still, I tried to make my appearance in the doorway as dramatic as possible, turning the corner and presenting myself with my arms held out to my sides so he could appreciate all my efforts.

"Wow." Matt stood up from the couch as he looked at me. Even Latte stood up, though he stayed on the couch. "You look amazing." He started to cross the room towards me.

"Is that what you're wearing?" The words spilled out of my mouth before I had the sense to swallow them down.

Matt looked down at his polo shirt and jeans. "I didn't realize you were going to be so dressed up."

"It's a gallery opening."

Matt looked at me blankly. "Do you want me to go change?" he asked finally.

Well, yes. "We'll be late."

"So what? At least we'll look good." He pecked me on the cheek and whispered in my ear, "You're beautiful," then hurried out the door.

I looked down at Latte, whose expression was already forlorn at his best buddy leaving. "You want to go outside?"

He jumped down from the couch and darted around me to stand anxiously at the door. He panted and stared at me intently. I opened the door, and he darted out into the dark.

It was decidedly on the chilly side, so I grabbed my dressy coat from the coatrack by the door and slipped it on. It may not have been the way I'd imagined the night starting, but that didn't mean the night as a whole was going to be a disappointment. I sighed. That's what I was going to tell myself anyway.

How did Matt not realize when I talked about a "date night" that it was supposed to be something special? Or when I took forever getting dressed instead of the five minutes I usually spent changing out of my work clothes and letting my hair down out of the chignon I kept it in to work at the coffee shop? Maybe it was my fault for not explicitly asking him to wear a suit. Which, I suddenly realized, I still hadn't asked him to do.

I looked up anxiously towards Matt's house. He was already jogging across our mutual neighbor's yard, thankfully in what at least looked like a sport jacket.

"Sorry!" He'd been working out the past couple of months and was only a little out of breath. That wasn't the only benefit–his arms were getting some nicely defined muscles too. "I got changed as fast as I could. If you can drive over, I can tie my tie in the car." He held up a tie as though to prove that he planned to put it on.

I looked him over, feeling a little bad for making him change. Well, I didn't make him, but I didn't exactly suggest that he didn't need to either. "Actually, I don't think you need the tie. You look nice like that." I reached out and smoothed his lapels affectionately. He really did look good without the tie. Handsome but boyish. Put-together but casual.

"Are you sure? Because I don't mind. I mean, I'm not going to complain about not wearing one, but–"

"I'm sure. Let's just get going."

"Okay." He shrugged. He balled up the tie and put it in his pocket.

"Latte!" I called him over from where he was sniffing the big oak tree in my yard. He looked at me for a second like maybe I just wanted to tell him something, like another good sniffing location. "Inside!" Good listener that he was, he immediately started trotting in our direction. He was almost inside when Matt stopped him.

"Here you go, buddy." He held out his hand, a treat nestled in his palm. Latte took it delicately then ran inside and straight up the stairs, where I would probably find him passed out on the bed when we got home in a few hours.

"Did you have that in your suit pocket?"

Matt grinned. "Sure did." He held his arm out for me to take. I slipped my hand under it, shaking my head and smiling to myself at how sweetly devoted my boyfriend was to my dog.

Five minutes later, we pulled up to the Cape Bay Museum of Art. The parking lot was the fullest I'd ever seen it. I wasn't sure if there were a lot of out-of-towners or if an unusually high number of Cape Bayers had decided to drive.

We made our way to the glass double doors leading into the museum, where a man with a clipboard was stationed.

"Name?" he asked, not quite rudely but not quite politely either, as we approached.

"Matt Cardosi," Matt said.

The man began scanning the list.

"It's under Francesca Amaro," I said before he could reject us.

He gave me a look—again, not quite rude but not quite polite—before looking back at his list. "Go ahead," he said after a few seconds, nodding curtly at the door.

Matt gave me a silent eyebrows-raised surprised look as he opened the door for me. I gave him a sympathetic eye roll and then called "Thank you!" back over my shoulder at the grump at the door. I thought I heard a grunt in reply.

Matt and I walked into the lobby. Based on the number of cars outside, I was surprised to see that it was empty except for one elderly man sitting on a couch off to one side of the room and a vaguely familiar-looking white-shirted bartender minding a table with an assortment of wine, beer, and—I leaned to see if that was what I thought it was.

"May I offer either of you a Goldschläger?" the bartender asked.

Yup. Cinnamon schnapps. It seemed like an odd choice for a gallery opening, especially since it was the only hard liquor they had.

"No," Matt said emphatically. "Beer, please!"

The bartender opened a beer and passed it to Matt. "And you, miss?"

"Nothing, thank you."

Matt looked at me, surprised.

I shrugged. "I want to have my hands free to look at the catalogue."

"Ready to go in then?"

I nodded.

We stepped past two security guards into the small hallway leading to the main gallery. A small pile of booklets sat on a table. I glanced at one, expecting it to be a list of upcoming exhibitions of the local schools' art, but was surprised to see that it was the exhibition catalogue. It was so small. A show for the likes of someone like Louis Cliffton would normally have what amounted to a coffee-table book for its catalogue. But this—this was practically nothing.

I picked it up and flipped to the first page to read the blurb about the show.

Gold. Silver. Diamonds. Rubies. For centuries, mankind has treasured these products of the earth, at times fighting and killing for them. Men have spent entire lifetimes trying to turn lead into gold, valuing the exquisite beauty of these materials above bread, above water, above flesh, above blood. While at times they have brought out humanity's best, they have also exposed our very worst.

For half a century, Louis Cliffton has held a mirror to humanity, reflecting back both what it did and didn't want to see. In Glimmer and Glare, Cliffton explores the materials we treasure above all things, from their beautiful glimmer to their destructive glare.

"What?" Matt asked from several steps ahead of me.

"Just reading the book." I didn't really know what to make of the introduction. I resisted the urge to turn the page to see the reproductions of the paintings, wanting to see them for the first time in real life.

I hurried up to Matt, and we turned the corner into the gallery space. It was packed with people. It seemed like Sammy was right, and not only had most of Cape Bay's elites and business owners been invited, but they'd all also accepted. On top of that, I recognized almost everyone. The few people I couldn't name, I recognized from the coffee shop. Apparently, the opening really was primarily for the people of Cape Bay. And they'd all driven.

I craned my neck to see the art on the walls. I could just catch a glimpse here and there between the crowds of people. Cape Bay wasn't a big town, but the gallery wasn't big either. When I finally managed to make my way to where I could actually see one of the artworks, I gasped.

I was sure it technically qualified as a painting—there was paint on the canvas, after all—but that certainly wasn't what drew my attention. Instead, my eyes fell on the melted gold that had been poured down the painting and the gemstones—actual gemstones—that had been embedded in it.

I looked around the room. Every painting had some kind of similar treatment—fine metals melted and poured or splashed across the canvas, jewels embedded in the metal or paint. Some had actual pieces of jewelry attached.

"Wow," Matt said beside me. "Think they're real?"

"Oh, they're real, all right," a voice said from my other side.

I turned to see Dean Howard, owner of the local jewelry store.

"Are you sure?"

"Matt, I've spent my life looking at jewelry. I can tell from across a room the color, cut, clarity, and carat of the diamond on a woman's finger. Most of the time, I can tell you if it's real or fake too. This stuff–" He gave a low whistle. "I'd hate to see what the insurance bills are on this. And the security they must have had to install. You pull the stuff off these, and most of it's gone forever. Completely untraceable. There's got to be almost a million dollars just in gold on these things."

"A Cliffton painting is worth quite a bit even without precious gems and metals on it," I said, a little defensively. For some reason, it bothered me to hear Cliffton's paintings reduced to the materials used to make them. Yes, the materials were the first thing that caught your eye when you came in the room, but once the initial shock wore off, it was clear that there was much more to the works in the exhibition than just their expensive components.

Cliffton was known for being an abstract expressionist—he made the kind of art people didn't really think was art—splatters of paint, large shapes, entire canvases painted in one color. And these were abstract and expressionist to be sure, with the metal and jewels fairly chaotic on the canvas, but when I started to look more closely, I realized that behind the finery were fully composed paintings. And not only that, some of them were replicas or near-replicas of famous paintings.

I saw Monet's Water Lilies, Van Gogh's self-portrait, Grant Wood's American Gothic, Whistler's mother, a Rembrandt, a Cezanne, a Gauguin. About half of the underlying paintings looked like something Cliffton himself would have painted and half looked like ones that almost anyone would recognize. Through a gap in the crowd, over in the corner, I even saw a painting that was a take on the Mona Lisa. Leaving Matt with Dean, I made my way over to it.

The painting was small like da Vinci's masterpiece, but the woman was turned to her left instead of her right, and she was blond instead of brunette. Her face was different too, rounder and more cherubic, but the color palette was the same. Even though it definitely wasn't the Mona Lisa, at the same time, it definitely was. And as small as it was, I was pretty sure it had more gold and gems on it than any other painting in the gallery.

Gold poured down the painting and puddled at the bottom. I stepped off to one side to confirm that, yes, there was so much gold at the bottom that it was three dimensional–the gold rose up off the canvas. And the gems! They looked like rain. There were a few sprinkled across the top then more as the gold poured down the side, then at the bottom, a virtual mountain of gems. They glimmered at me as I moved back and forth, watching the effect. It was almost too much. It was almost tacky.

But somehow it wasn't. And then I realized why. I only noticed it as I moved back and forth. Out of the woman's eye, down her cheek, was the thinnest strand of gold–so thin you could only see it when the light hit it. A tear. Suddenly I was overtaken by the beauty of the painting. And something else–the sadness. And then I thought of my mother, and tears sprang to my eyes. This was going to be my first Thanksgiving without her.

"Do you like it?" a Boston accent asked from off to my right.

I nodded, not wanting to look over and let whoever it was see that I was on the verge of tears.

"It's my mother."

Now I looked. Beside me was Louis Cliffton.

"The *Mona Lisa* always reminded me of her a bit—beautiful, but enigmatic. Always seeming to know something no one else did."

I wondered if I'd somehow known that the painting was of his mother and that's why it had reminded me of my own.

"She died over the summer."

I'd turned back to the painting but snapped my head back to look at him. "Your mother?"

He nodded.

"Mine too."

"Perhaps that's why you connected so deeply with it."

"Perhaps." I stared at the painting again. I don't know if it was because Cliffton was beside me, but its sadness felt like a real, physical thing now.

"I painted the portrait before she died and then added the decoration afterward. I would have continued the series," he said, waving his hand around the gallery, "but I put everything I had left into this."

I knew he meant the gold and jewels, but I wondered if he didn't also mean emotionally.

"It's beautiful."

He nodded soberly, agreeing like it wasn't a compliment but an objective fact, which I guess it was. The painting was objectively beautiful.

"I heard your mother grew up here?" I asked, after spending another moment taking the painting in.

"She did. Just down the street, actually. Having this show here seemed like a fitting tribute to her."

"Hey, there you are!" Matt slipped his arm around my waist and kissed my temple.

"Mr. Cliffton, this is my boyfriend, Matt Cardosi. Matt, this is Louis Cliffton, the artist. This is his show."

"It's a pleasure to meet you, Mr. Cliffton," Matt said, stepping forward to shake his hand. "I've never seen anything quite like your, uh, artworks." I could tell Matt didn't know quite how to refer to Cliffton's nontraditional collection.

"Indeed." Cliffton nodded as he shook Matt's hand. Then he turned to me. "And your name?"

"Oh!" I was a little embarrassed that I hadn't thought to introduce myself, even when I was introducing him and Matt. "I'm Francesca. Francesca Amaro. I own Antonia's Italian Café down on Main Street. We've been in Cape Bay for almost seventy years. Well, not me obviously, but my family. My grandparents started the café. We'd love to have you in while you're in town." And now I was embarrassed that I was chattering on about my small family café to a world-famous artist.

"Did you say Antonia's?"

"Yes." Apparently, I wasn't even enunciating properly as I chattered.

A smile spread across Cliffton's face, lighting up his eyes. "My mother used to work there."

"Really?" I instantly felt better.

"When she was in school. She was very particular about her coffee as a result of her time there."

"It is a known side effect of working there."

Cliffton chuckled before looking somewhere over my shoulder. "If you'll excuse me, my assistant is looking for me. It was a pleasure to meet both of you. And Francesca, expect to see me in your café tomorrow." He patted me on the shoulder before walking off across the room.

I turned to see who his assistant was. It was the grouchy man from the door. I was both surprised and not at the same time. I would have expected such a famous artist's assistant to have more manners than the man had exhibited, but I could also see how he might be less than thrilled to be in Cape Bay as compared to the more cosmopolitan locales he was probably used to.

The two men appeared to already be engaged in an intense conversation. The assistant was gesturing broadly while

Cliffton was mostly still, but his face was stern. The assistant gesticulated, then Cliffton silenced him with a word or two. The assistant stared at him. Before I could see what happened next, Matt brushed his hand against my arm.

"Mary Ellen's talking to you."

I turned to see Mary Ellen Chapman, owner of the town's best and main souvenir and gift shop, standing next to me. "I'm sorry, Mary Ellen, what did you say?"

"I asked how you liked the exhibition."

"I love it," I replied.

When I glanced back over my shoulder to check on Cliffton and his assistant, they were both gone.

Chapter Four

That night, I couldn't sleep. I had been distracted through the rest of the evening, and when we got home from dinner, I'd told Matt that I needed some time alone and sent him home. I lay in bed for nearly an hour, staring at the ceiling, unable to get my mind off Cliffton's portrait of his mother. It was so beautifully done and so extravagant and so sad.

I thought about how Cliffton had taken all the supplies he had left for his entire *Glimmer and Glare* series and dumped them on that one canvas, how the series had effectively stopped with his mother's death, how my life had effectively stopped with my mother's death.

I decided I needed a cup of herbal tea. Sleepless nights were the one time I diverged from my coffee habit. I made my way downstairs, Latte tripping at my heels, excited to find out why we were doing something so unusual as getting out of bed before the sun came up.

I sat at the kitchen table, my mug of tea warming my hands, my dog warming my feet, for a few minutes before I decided that it was as good a time as any to work on my menu for Thanksgiving. I had most of the dinner figured out except for dessert. Everyone I'd invited had offered to bring something, many of them offering pies of various types, but I still wanted to make at least one dessert myself. I wouldn't feel like a proper hostess otherwise.

I wanted to look online for recipes, but my phone and computer were both upstairs in my bedroom. It would be easy enough to go up and get them, but once I got upstairs, I would feel like I should try again to sleep, and I knew my brain wouldn't go for that. I sat there for a few more minutes until my eyes fell on the collection of cookbooks in the corner of the kitchen. My mother's cookbooks. I hadn't touched them since her death, hadn't wanted to. I'd only ever used them when making something with her, and I was never going to make anything with her again.

But I missed her. And in that moment, I thought that maybe if I flipped through their pages, I'd feel like she was there with me again.

I stood up, crossed the room, grabbed a cookbook without looking, and brought it back to the table with me. I looked at the cover. *American Pies: 50 Classic Recipes.* I knew this cookbook. It was one of my mother's favorites, especially around the holidays.

I flipped the pages back and forth then let the book open to whatever page it wanted. It was exactly the page I knew it would be. Apple Pie. My mother's favorite. She'd baked this pie at least twice every fall.

I read down the page, remembering going through each of the steps with her. By the time I got to the words "Slice and enjoy!" I knew I was going to make a pie. And not in the morning either. Now.

I got up from the table, startling Latte, who watched me long enough to determine that it wasn't breakfast time before going back to sleep. I moved quickly around the kitchen, gathering the ingredients I needed. I worked my way through the recipe, preparing the dough for the crust before putting it in the refrigerator to chill and rest. Then I set to making the filling. When that was done, I assembled the pie, put it in the oven, and anxiously waited to "Slice and enjoy!"

The finished pie was terrible. The crust was dense and a little soggy. I wasn't satisfied or tired, so I made another one. That time, I messed up the filling, so I made another. And another. Fortunately, Matt and I had gone apple picking the week before and I had a really large stock of apples. Too many, really. Unless, of course, you're going to make five pies in a night. Which I did. And the fifth one was perfect. Exactly like the ones my mother used to make.

My brain calmed, I climbed the stairs to my bedroom. The last thing I thought as my head hit the pillow was that I should make more pies and sell them in the café.

Chapter Five

I woke up later that morning to see Latte's face a quarter inch away from mine. I could barely focus my eyes on his face, it was so close.

"Good morning," I croaked.

He panted happily and licked my face.

"I guess you want breakfast." I rolled over onto my back. Latte took that as an invitation to use me as a pillow and climbed on top of me. I scratched his head. He licked my face again.

It wasn't all that much later than I usually got up—about an hour, give or take—but given that the sun had already been peeking over the horizon when I went to bed, I was still pretty tired. My eyes felt like they were made of sandpaper. If I could just close my eyes for a few more minutes...

Latte bumped my nose with his. "Okay, okay. But you have to get off me first."

Latte wiggled over onto the bed almost immediately, as if he understood what I'd said. I rolled over onto my other side and grabbed my phone, wanting to delay getting out of bed just a few more minutes. My only notifications were a couple of emails promoting sales on websites I'd made purchases from five or so years ago and one text from Matt that came in while I was baking. I'd collapsed into bed when I came upstairs without so much as glancing at my phone, so I hadn't seen it.

Had fun with you last night. Hope you're feeling better after getting some rest

I tapped a message back one-handed.

Didn't get much sleep, but I am feeling better. PS—I have pie

I'd kept all the failed pies. They were edible, just not good. But I knew Matt would be happy to eat them. And if he didn't like one, there was another one he could try.

Latte flopped down on top of me, apparently tired of waiting.

"Okay, okay," I muttered. I wiggled out from under him and sat up on the side of the bed. It was chilly outside of the covers. I hurried to pull on a sweatshirt and some sweatpants and made my way downstairs. Latte narrowly avoided tripping me as he darted around my feet.

I opened the back door to let him out while I got his food. It was even colder outside. I should have expected that, but I still shrank back into the house and went to turn the heat up. On the way to the thermostat, I glanced at the clock. I'd been hoping to go back by the museum to look at the portrait of Cliffton's mother on my way into the café, but Latte had let me sleep too late. Oh, well. It would be there for two weeks. I had plenty of time to go see it again.

I put some food into Latte's bowl, let him back inside, and made myself a cup of coffee. A cappuccino, actually. A very big cappuccino. My coffee machine at home obviously wasn't nearly as fancy as the one at the café, but it was still a lot nicer than most people's. It could grind the coffee beans for me, make espresso, steam milk, and do everything else I needed to make coffee for just one or two people. It was even connected to the house's water, so I never had to refill it.

The hot cup felt good in my cold hands. I took my first sip. Perfection. It might take me five tries to make a perfect pie, but coffee I could practically do in my sleep. In fact, once in college, my roommate woke me up in the middle of the night to make her a cup of coffee to help her get through an all-nighter. She told me the next morning that she didn't think I'd ever actually opened my eyes while I was doing it.

Once the coffee had gotten me reasonably warmed and woken up, I went upstairs to get myself dressed. Half an hour later, I took Latte for a walk around the block, packed up my one really good pie, and headed in to the café.

I took the shortcut I used to take as a kid. Out the back door, through my backyard and a few others, then down the block and in through the back door of Antonia's. I could hear Sammy and Becky out front, sounding like they had everything under control.

I stayed in the back room and worked on getting it straightened up. It wasn't messy, but there were a few dishes that needed to be washed, a few that needed to be put away, and a few odds and ends that needed to be attended to. Typical stuff for that time of day. We didn't have a huge lunch rush, but it was enough that things started to get a little behind.

I was just finishing up when Sammy popped in. She jumped when she saw me. "Geez, Fran! You scared me! I didn't hear you come in."

"Sorry." I'd thought about popping my head out to let them know I'd arrived but decided against it. Apparently, I decided wrong.

"I just need to grab some napkins." At least she was quick to forgive.

The box was next to me, so I handed some to her. It seemed like we were always restocking the napkins. I'd tried to think of a way to avoid having to do it so often, but I didn't want to just leave stacks of them out front, and that was the only alternative I could come up with. We already had them at the counter and on all the tables. We just went through that many of them.

"Thanks." She half turned to leave then stopped and looked at me with her eyes narrowed like she was trying to figure something out. "I have to talk to you later. When things slow down a little."

Something about the way she said it made me a little uneasy. I hoped no one was dead. We'd had an awful lot of murders lately in Cape Bay. I momentarily wondered if I should ask, but I decided I probably would have heard if something happened to someone close to me. And Sammy would be crying. She wasn't good at holding back her tears.

"Okay," I replied, still a little hesitant. She was halfway out the door when I realized I wasn't being a very good boss or coworker. "Hey, do you guys need help out there?"

"You know we can always use an extra pair of hands. But we have everything under control if you still have stuff to do back here." She stopped and looked from the pie I'd left on the table to me and back to the pie. "Is that what I think it is?"

"A pie?" I wasn't sure why she had to ask. It was pretty obvious it was.

"An apple pie?" She looked like she was about to break into a grin.

It wasn't an off-the-wall guess—it wasn't peach cobbler season or anything—but I was still a little surprised that she guessed the flavor right. Actually, what surprised me was probably that she seemed so confident about it. "How did you know?"

That was definitely a grin on her face. "It's what your mom always made." She glanced around the room. "Is that your sample? I was wondering when you didn't bring one to our taste test, but I didn't want to bring it up in case it was a sensitive subject. Everyone will be so excited! They've been asking–" She stopped and stared at me for a second. "You didn't know?"

"Know what?" I asked cautiously.

"That your mom used to sell them this time of year. They were always really popular. People would even buy them to serve at their Thanksgiving dinners."

I stared at her, tears pricking at my eyes. "I had no idea."

"Oh. I'm sorry if I–"

I shook my head. "No, it's okay. You're fine. I just, um–" I shook my head again.

"You just wanted to bring in an apple pie, and I had to go and make it about your mom. I'm sorry. I shouldn't have said anything about selling them."

"No, that's the thing—" I took a deep breath to try to calm myself down. "I wanted to sell them. I just didn't know my mom used to."

"Is it her recipe?"

I nodded. "I couldn't sleep last night. I kept thinking about her after we got home from the gallery opening and dinner. I finally got up and was looking through one of her old cookbooks when I saw the apple pie recipe and decided to make one. It took me five tries to get it right, but once I did, I decided that we should sell them. In her memory."

"Without even knowing that she used to."

I fought back tears as I nodded.

"It was meant to be."

I nodded again.

Sammy waited for a few seconds while I struggled to regain my composure. "Do you want me to take that one out there?" she asked finally. "It'll go fast."

I shook my head vigorously. "I already cut into it to see how it came out."

"Well then, how about Becky and I get things settled down out there, and then we can come back here, and you can let us try it?"

I nodded.

"That'll give you some time to"–she looked at me and then around the perfectly neat room–"get things cleaned up back here. Sound good?"

"Sounds good." I forced a smile.

"Sammy, do you have those napkins?" Becky called from out front.

"Yup, just a second!" Sammy called back. "Duty calls." She smiled at me and left with the napkins.

I sank down in the closest chair. I was surprised by how emotional I'd gotten and how quickly. I thought I'd dealt with my mother's death, but here it was, sneaking up on me when I least expected it. Maybe it was the holidays coming up. They'd be my first on my own. Matt's first on his own too, although I seemed to recall that his dad never really made a big deal out of the season.

Gino Cardosi hadn't been what I would call a festive man. After Matt's mom died when we were kids, my family used to have Matt and his dad over for holiday meals. That stopped after my grandparents passed away though. It didn't really surprise me. My grandparents had had a soft spot for Mr. Cardosi as a fellow Italian immigrant and a high tolerance for his curmudgeonly behavior. My mother? Not so much.

Whether it was to avoid spending the holidays with him or just to get away from the memories, after my grandparents were gone, my mother took to travelling for the holidays. She'd go somewhere warm and exotic and distant. I joined her when I could, but it wasn't often. I didn't get much time off, especially since that was the time of year when my celebrity PR clients seemed particularly inclined to crash their cars into trees or get caught cheating on their spouses. Nothing ruins a relaxing Thanksgiving on the beach like a cabana boy delivering a message from your boss saying that you need to get back to the States *now* because your biggest client and his angry wife are leading off the nightly news.

I was happy I was a simple café owner in a resort town on the beach in Massachusetts now. The worst calamity I might have to deal with over the holidays was a massive snow storm.

I glanced over at the pie on the table. I'd had no idea that my mother used to sell that pie in the café. I hadn't even planned on selling it when I'd started my furious pie-baking marathon the night before—I'd just wanted to do something that would make me feel close to my mother. It was an urge I'd felt ever since I laid eyes on Cliffton's amazing portrait of his own mother at the show the night before.

I was halfway annoyed with myself for sleeping so late that I couldn't make it to the museum to see the painting again before coming in to the café. At the same time, I knew that I couldn't possibly have dragged myself out of bed any earlier than I did after staying up all night baking—despite my massive cup of coffee, my eyelids were already getting heavy. It was a shame that the museum would be closed when I left the café for the night.

And then I realized that I didn't actually know that it would be. It wouldn't normally even cross my mind that they could be open so late—not that it was all that late—especially when it wasn't tourist season, but with the Cliffton show in town, I wondered if they might be keeping special hours.

I grabbed my handbag from the drawer I'd tucked it in. I'd taken it to the opening the night before. I didn't remember seeing the catalogue from the show anywhere in my house, so it was either in my bag or in Matt's car. I opened the Italian leather bag up and dug through its contents. The booklet was in Matt's car.

I was momentarily disappointed before I realized that it was the twenty-first century and most places had websites. Even Antonia's had a website, although it needed a lot of modernizing. I made a mental note to find someone to help me with that and went over to the computer.

I wasn't sure of the museum's web address, so I typed "Cape Bay Museum of Art" in the search bar.

Instead of the museum's website being the first result, several news articles showed up at the top of the screen. While it wasn't what I expected, I wasn't really surprised. A full show of a new collection from an artist the caliber of Cliffton would certainly make the news.

And then I saw what the headlines said.

Heist of the Century? Priceless Cliffton Painting Stolen from Cape Bay Museum of Art

Glimmer and Gone: Cliffton Painting Stolen on Opening Night

Opening Nightmare: Cliffton's Masterpiece Stolen from Cape Bay, Mass., Museum

I stared dumbly at the computer screen, not believing what I saw and hoping against hope that the "priceless masterpiece" of the collection wasn't what I thought it was.

I clicked on the first article.

Directly under the headline, I could see the very top part of an image—not enough to know what it was. I hovered my hand over the mouse, afraid of what I'd see if I scrolled down. Finally, I took a deep breath and slid the mouse down.

The portrait of Cliffton's mother was gone.

Chapter Six

It couldn't be true.

I stared at the screen. The picture on it was definitely the *Mona Lisa*-inspired portrait of Cliffton's mother. I read the caption.

Glimmer No. 7: The painting by Louis Cliffton, stolen last night from the Cape Bay Museum of Art in Cape Bay, Massachusetts.

I felt a faint bit of hope disappear. I hadn't realized until that moment that some little part of me thought that maybe a different painting had been taken and this one was just illustrating the article. I scrolled down to the article.

My eyes skimmed the page. "Museum gallery opening... renowned artist Louis

Cliffton... Glimmer and Glare, adorned with gold, silver, and gems... painting inspired by his mother... stolen during the night... Detective Michael Stanton of the Cape Bay Police Department declined comment."

Mike. Of course he was assigned to the case. In Cape Bay's tiny police department, he was pretty much the be-all and end-all of investigations. This case would attract national attention though. I hoped he was prepared for that.

I went back to skimming the article. It was generic boilerplate, the bare bones of a report from a small town. The bit about Mike was the only thing that looked like someone had done anything beyond read that the painting had been stolen and then add a few details they found online about the town and Cliffton. I could find out more by going out into the café and asking what everybody knew. Because, of course, they knew. In a town the size of Cape Bay, everyone knew everything. The only reason I didn't was because the only person I'd seen so far was Sammy, and she—well, I didn't know why she didn't tell me.

I listened for the sounds coming from the café. It sounded like it was still on the busy side. I'd have to ask her later.

I clicked the back button on the browser and went down to the next article in the list. It was more of the same. Back again and on to the next one. I was about to dismiss that one as well when something caught my eye.

Adam Shuster, owner of the museum, said that while the theft was a tragedy, he hoped no one would be dissuaded from coming to the show. "We're going to reopen as soon as the police give me the go ahead, so everyone who wants to come should still plan on coming. The show is amazing even without the painting that was stolen, and we have an amazing collection of other art from artists across New England." Shuster recommends checking the museum's website for updates about when it will reopen to the public.

So Adam owned the museum now. I don't know why it hadn't occurred to me before that he would. His parents had been getting up there in years back when I was growing up. It made sense that he would be in charge now. And it explained why everything was so run-down. Adam had a reputation around town of being rather lazy and shiftless. I'd heard the phrase "riding on his parents' coattails" more than once in reference to him. My mother had never been a fan of him despite, or perhaps because of, growing up with him. She'd always said he'd run the museum into the ground if he ever was in control of it. Apparently, she was right. She usually was.

I drummed my fingers on the desk. Something about the article bothered me, but I couldn't put my finger on what it was. It was the same as the other articles in every way except the quote from Adam. So what was it that wasn't sitting right?

"Ready for some apple pie?"

I turned around to see Sammy and Becky standing just inside the room.

"What're you looking at?" Sammy asked, taking the three steps over to me. "Oh."

"You knew?"

She nodded. "People were talking about it all morning. I was going to tell you, but I wanted to wait until things were less busy."

That was fair. After all, she had said she wanted to tell me something.

"Did you see that one last night?"

I looked back at the computer screen and scrolled up just a little to get the whole painting in the frame. "Yes. It was... stunning."

"Hard to believe it happened in Cape Bay."

I thought for a second. "Is it though? It's not like the stuff our museum usually has. I mean, Louis Cliffton has paintings in the Museum of Modern Art. They sell for millions of dollars. I can kind of see why an art thief would think it was an easy target here."

"But Ryan told me they had a bunch of security for the show!"

"They did?" I thought back to the museum the night before. I vaguely remembered a couple of security guards at the entrance to the gallery but nothing else. Of course, good security would be mostly invisible. "Did Ryan tell you what kind of security they had?"

"It sounded like a lot of stuff. Lasers, motion sensors, cameras. Mike was in charge of all of it. You could ask him if you wanted to know exactly."

I gave her a look. "Really? You think Mike wants me, of all people, asking him about the security system that he set up that didn't keep an incredibly valuable painting from being stolen the first night it was there?"

Sammy thought for a second and then grimaced. "Yeah, I guess not."

Mike and I were friends. We'd known each other since we were kids. But I'd gotten myself involved in a couple of murder investigations over the past few months, and while I'd at the very least helped solve all of them, he hadn't exactly appreciated my interference. I had a feeling that any questions I started asking about the art theft wouldn't exactly be greeted with enthusiasm.

"Do you want me to ask Ryan?" Sammy offered. "I'm going to see him—I mean, I'm sure he'll be in sometime. You know how he likes his coffee."

Yeah, I thought, *his coffee and the girl serving it.* I thought better of saying that out loud. "No, don't worry about it. I'm staying out of this one."

"That's what you always say."

"Should I go back out front?" Becky asked, still hovering in the doorway.

Sammy and I had completely forgotten the apple pie while we talked about the stolen painting.

"Oh! No, come have a seat." I slid the wheeled office chair across the floor to the pie and took the foil off. Except for the one narrow slice I'd tasted early that morning, it was perfect. "It would be better if it was hot, but I didn't even think about putting it in the warmer."

"I'm sure it's delicious the way it is," Sammy said, grabbing a chair and pulling it up to the table. She turned and grabbed some plates and forks from the shelf and laid them out for us.

Becky pulled up another chair and sat down as I started to cut into the pie. I sliced three pieces and laid them out on the plates. "Dig in!"

I watched and waited as they each took their first bite. What if the pie had taken the same turn for the worse after cooling as the spicy pumpkin flaxseed branola cookies and it was inedible now? What if I'd just been so exhausted that morning after cooking five pies that my brain had just decided that whatever I put into my mouth was delicious?

"This is really good, Fran!" Sammy said, a smile spreading across her face.

I exhaled a sigh of relief.

Becky nodded enthusiastically. "Mm-hmm, I really like it," she said around a mouthful of pie.

"Great!" I felt like I'd done my mother proud. I took a bite of my slice of pie. It really was good. Even better than when it was fresh out of the oven. Well, that, or I was actually awake enough to taste the spices in it and appreciate the perfect flakiness of the crust up against the soft texture of the apple filling. I went back for another bite then finished off the slice.

The bell over the café door jingled, and Sammy went out to help the customer. She'd barely stepped out of the room when I heard her say, much more loudly than necessary, "Oh, hello, Ryan, *Mike*."

I rolled my eyes. I knew what she was doing.

"Is she okay?" Becky asked. "Did she say it like that because she wants me to go out and help her?"

"No." I sighed heavily as I stood up. "She thinks I should go out there and talk to Mike about the painting that was stolen."

"Hey, Fran! Mike and Ryan are here!"

Becky giggled.

"I heard! Do you need help?" I called back to her, just to see how hard she'd push to get me to go out there.

"No, I just thought you said something about wanting to talk to Mike."

I sighed and shook my head. "She has no shame," I said quietly to Becky. She giggled again.

From out in the café, I heard a low rumble that sounded like Mike's voice, followed by Sammy's laugh and something from Ryan. If I had to guess, I would have said Mike was preemptively complaining about me sticking my nose in his business.

"Guess I better go out there," I said.

"I'm scheduled to leave now. Is it okay if I go?" Becky asked before I could leave the room.

"Yes, that's fine."

"Can I take a couple slices of apple pie for my mom? It's her favorite."

"Sure. And let her know we'll start selling them tomorrow if she wants more."

"I will! She'll probably want some for Thanksgiving!"

I had a feeling a lot of people would. I said goodbye to Becky and went out into the café. I grabbed a large to-go cup as I passed them and walked straight to the pot of freshly brewed black coffee. I filled the cup as close to the brim as I could without spilling it and put the lid on. I turned around and handed it directly to Mike.

"Buttering me up?"

Ryan and Sammy laughed.

"Nope. I just know you that well."

He grunted and took a sip then nodded. I took that as a sign of approval and gratitude.

"I heard a painting was stolen from the art museum last night," Sammy said.

I glared at her. Ryan laughed, and I glared at him too.

"You know, if you're that bored, I have plenty of misdemeanors you could nose around on. You don't have to wait around for the felonies. Petty crime would plummet as soon as all the teenage vandals found out you'd be the one after them."

Sometimes with Mike, I couldn't tell whether or not he was joking. In this case, I didn't see why anyone would ever be more threatened by me than Mike, but maybe I underestimated how much power I had as the primary purveyor of the town's coffee.

We did have a pretty decent after-school rush with all the high schoolers coming in to order their excessively elaborate drinks. We went through more syrup in that one half-hour period than in the entire rest of the day. Sometimes I wondered what it would take to get them to appreciate a simple, well-made latte.

"Don't worry," I said. "I'm not getting involved."

Mike grunted. I took that as a sign he didn't believe me.

"Really," I said. "I have enough to do getting ready for Thanksgiving. Which reminds me, do you know yet if you and Sandra are coming?"

"Her parents rented a cabin in the mountains, so we're going up there."

"That sounds fun!"

Ryan made a noise that sounded like a snort, and Mike shot a look in his direction. Ryan looked down at his coffee, but I saw him peek over it and wink at Sammy. I looked at Mike as though none of that had just happened.

"Sandra has eight nieces and nephews," he said.

"Oh, wow."

"Under ten years old."

"Oh. Wow." When you added in Mike and Sandra's two kids, that was ten children under ten years old.

"And they all have dogs."

I wrinkled my forehead. "All eight kids?"

Mike looked at me like I was crazy. "No. Well, I guess." He shook his head. "Whatever. Their parents. And Sandra's parents. It's like five dogs, last time I counted." He looked disgusted, even though I knew one of the dogs was his.

"So, it sounds like you're looking forward to it!" I joked.

"I'm looking forward to spending most of my time in the woods."

"Hunting?"

"Enjoying the silence."

I unsuccessfully tried to hide my laugh. I expected Mike to glare at me, but instead the corners of his eyes crinkled.

"It's a lot of kids, Franny."

I laughed for real that time.

Before either of us could say anything else, the radio on Ryan's shoulder crackled to life. The person on the other end talked so fast and in so much police jargon, I couldn't understand what they were saying. Ryan said something back into it. All I could make out of that was "10-4."

"Looks like we gotta go," he said to us. "Thanks for the coffee, Sam." He paused for a second then added, "And Fran."

"Anytime," I replied as Sammy blushed. I wondered exactly who they thought was fooled by their "we're not together" act.

"Thanks, Fran," Mike said, tipping his cup in my direction. "Keep working on that Thanksgiving planning. I don't want to hear anything about you playing investigator."

"You don't have to worry about me!"

Mike looked skeptical but didn't say anything as he headed for the door.

As he and Ryan left the café, I caught sight of a man sitting at a table by the window, typing furiously on his laptop. Something about him looked familiar, but I couldn't place him until he looked up from his computer and wrinkled his forehead, looking annoyed.

"Sammy!" I whispered.

"What?"

"That man. Over by the window."

She looked. "What about him?"

"That's Louis Cliffton's assistant! I recognize him from the opening last night!"

"Are you sure?" Sammy leaned to get a better angle to see him. "He doesn't look like an artist's assistant."

"What does an artist's assistant look like?"

"I dunno. Like an artist but more–" She hesitated thoughtfully. "Assistanty?"

I almost asked what an artist looked like but decided it wouldn't be productive. Instead, I looked Cliffton's assistant over. He had short hair, but not cop-short like Mike's and Ryan's. His cut was the kind of short that looked unimpressive but that I could tell was very expensive. He wore wire-frame glasses, a white button-down shirt, tan slacks, and a tweed–yes, tweed– jacket, complete with elbow patches. I had to admit, he did look more like an adjunct English professor than the assistant of a world-renowned artist.

"I'm going to go over and talk to him," I said, still whispering.

"I thought you told Mike you were staying out of it."

"I am," I said, stepping around the counter. "I'm just going over to say hello." And at the time, I meant it.

Chapter Seven

"How is everything?" I asked, walking up to Cliffton's assistant's table.

He didn't look up from his computer.

"Excuse me, sir?"

Now he looked up at me. I was a little surprised that he didn't look annoyed, I guess because he'd looked annoyed most of the time that I'd seen him. I wasn't sure what to make of the expression on his face. It was really almost blank to the point that I wondered if he was fully aware that I was standing there. I put on my best café-owner smile.

"How is everything? Are you enjoying your coffee?"

He looked down at his mostly empty cup of coffee and the half-eaten muffin beside it.

I waited.

"Yes, it's very good," he said finally. He whipped off his glasses one-handed like he was some debonair character in a movie and leaned back in his chair. "Sorry if I'm a little distracted. I was lost in my novel."

"Oh, you're writing a novel?" I tried to sound as interested as I could. It wasn't that I wasn't interested, it was just that he seemed particularly concerned that I know he was writing a novel.

He slung one arm over the back of the chair and smiled. "I am. It's quite an epic. Don't be surprised if you see the name Brent Griffin on the bestseller lists."

Nothing like deciding that the book you were still in the middle of writing was a bestseller. "That's you? Brent Griffin?"

"That's me."

I'd been planning to just identify him outright as Cliffton's assistant, but he was selling the writer thing so hard that I was starting to wonder if I'd been wrong and he wasn't Cliffton's assistant after all. So I decided to play dumb. I wrinkled my forehead and studied him for a second, like I was trying to figure something out. "Weren't you at the Cliffton opening last night?"

He hesitated for just a second, and I thought I saw his expression momentarily darken. It was so slight and so brief though that it could have just been a cloud passing in front of the sun outside. "I was," he said finally.

"I thought so!" I knew I might still be wrong about him being Cliffton's assistant, but at least I was right about seeing him at the museum the night before. "Didn't I see you talking to him?"

There was that hesitation again. I didn't wait for it to pass this time though.

"Do you know him?"

Brent shifted uncomfortably in his chair. All the swagger he'd been oozing seconds before was gone. "I'm, uh, his assistant."

I knew it! But he seemed less interested in talking now that he'd admitted it. I had to keep him going. I didn't even know why. I pulled out the chair across from him and sat down. "Mind if I sit down? That must be so interesting, being the assistant to a famous artist!"

He scowled.

"No?"

"Only if you like being condescended to."

That surprised me. It had been obvious that he was less interested in talking about Cliffton—or probably anything—than his novel, but I hadn't expected him to be so disdainful about it. "Is he unpleasant to work for?"

"He just treats me like I'm less than him. Like he's so special because he's the artist, and I'm just some nobody who's there to answer his emails."

I wouldn't have put it into quite those words, and I would never say it to Brent, but that sounded like the definition of an assistant to me. I said the most sympathetic-sounding thing that came to mind: "That's such a shame."

"You're telling me. I didn't go to graduate school to be treated like someone's servant."

Again, that sounded like the definition of an assistant, but I still wasn't going to say it.

"But I won't be for much longer."

"Are you getting a new job?" I asked.

"Of course." He smiled and waved his hand at his computer. "This."

"Writing?"

"That's right."

"Well, congratulations!" Maybe he was further along with his book than I thought. "You already have a publisher?"

"Not yet. I'm still in the writing process." He looked at me meaningfully. "Like I said, it's an epic."

"I see." I didn't really, but I assumed it meant the book was going to be very long and he wasn't anywhere near done with it yet. "But you're ready to quit and write full time?"

He nodded then glanced around and leaned in towards me. "A, uh, relative passed away, and I'm going to be coming into some money." He held a single finger to his lips in the universal "shh" sign.

"Your secret is safe with me," I said quietly.

He smiled and winked at me then picked up his glasses from where he'd laid them on the table. "But I should be getting back to work. The great American novel doesn't write itself."

I realized I hadn't talked to him about the stolen painting. Not that I came over looking for leads in the case or anything. I was just curious to hear what Cliffton's assistant would have to say about it.

To be honest, I'd expected him to be more distraught over the matter. With all the typing he was doing, I thought maybe he was working on insurance documents or something, not working on his novel like his boss hadn't just had a major work of art stolen. It was an impressive level of disconnect, even for somebody who hated his job.

But what if he didn't know yet about the theft? It didn't seem likely, especially not with all of Cape Bay buzzing about it and the story being national news. On the other hand, maybe he really hated working for Cliffton so much that he really wasn't bothered that the painting was gone.

Whatever the case, I wasn't going to earn any goodwill by sitting there and making him talk about it when he clearly wanted to get back to his writing. Instead, I'd just have to make sure I had the chance to talk about it with him in the future.

"I'll leave you alone so you can concentrate," I said as I stood up. "Please let me or Sammy over there know if you need anything else—more coffee, another muffin. Your next drink is on the house."

"Thank you," he said, beaming up at me.

"I'm Francesca Amaro, by the way," I said, sticking my hand out. He shook it. "I'm the owner. Feel free to stop in anytime while you're in town. You're welcome to stay and write as long as you'd like."

"Well, thank you, Francesca. And it's a pleasure to meet you."

"You can call me Fran."

"But Francesca is such a beautiful name. You don't mind if I call you that, do you?"

"No, not at all."

"Great. *Francesca*," he repeated. "I may have to find a way to work that name into my book. *Francesca*." He pushed his glasses onto his face and turned back to his computer. I took that as my cue to leave.

I made my way nonchalantly around the café and back over to Sammy, picking up the detritus of the lunch rush as I went.

"Get any good info on the stolen painting?" she whispered when I walked around the counter.

"Didn't even ask," I replied, more than a little self-righteously.

"Really? Then what did you talk about?"

I paused for a second. "His novel. And how much he hates working for Cliffton."

Sammy seemed to have to think about that. "He's writing a novel?"

I nodded. "He very much wants to talk about it."

"I thought he looked a little pretentious."

I stifled a laugh. Some of it slipped out, but Brent was so engrossed in his novel that he didn't seem to notice.

"And he hates working for Cliffton, huh?"

"Yup. Doesn't like being treated like he's just there to assist the artist."

Now it was Sammy's turn to laugh. "You know, that's what I've always hated about working here–the way you expect me to work here."

I looked at her sharply for a second. She was joking, right? I didn't treat her poorly, did I?

"Relax, Fran!" she said and elbowed me playfully. "I work here, that's the point. You treat me like an employee because I am one."

"But you're my friend too! I don't treat you guys poorly, do I?" I tried to think of whether I'd accidentally been rude or unkind to any of them lately. They worked for me, but I didn't want them to think I didn't appreciate them.

"Fran, I was joking! You're great! Your mom was great! Your grandparents were great! If anything, I'd say you make me feel like I'm almost as important around here as you are."

"Sammy, you are."

She gave me a look like she didn't believe me.

"No, really. Without you, I would have to be here first thing in the morning to open up every day. I wouldn't have remembered that pumpkin spice lattes should be on the menu. I *would have served those spicy pumpkin flaxseed branola cookies.*"

Sammy laughed. "You would have figured out how bad they were when people started spitting them out."

"I would have been so bleary eyed from lack of sleep that I probably wouldn't have noticed."

A customer came in, and Sammy moved over to the register to take her order. I took the lunch dishes I'd gathered up into the back room.

"So you didn't ask him about the stolen painting at all, huh? I'm impressed," Sammy said after the customer had her drink.

I shrugged. "I wanted to. Not because I want to figure out who took it, but because I just want to talk about that painting. You should have seen it, Sammy. It was... incredible."

"I saw the pictures online. Was that real gold on it?"

"Pictures don't do it justice. And, yes, it was real gold. And real gems. I couldn't believe how much he used. The whole series had them, but that one—he said there would have been more paintings, but he used everything he had left on it."

Sammy stood and looked thoughtful for a minute. "Do you think it was stolen for the gold and gems? Like, to scrape them off the painting and sell them?"

I stared at her in horror. The thought hadn't even occurred to me. The idea that someone would destroy that exquisite painting just for the—admittedly incredibly expensive—materials used to make it was horrifying to me. And the thought that I might never see it again—it made me want to cry. Not just because it was beautiful, but because it made me think of my mother. And then to think that it was a portrait of Cliffton's mother—one he had put so much time and effort into, and now he might never see it again. I hoped Mike already had a lead in the case. Maybe if he caught the person fast enough, they wouldn't have the chance to destroy the painting. I couldn't stand the thought of it being destroyed.

"I hope not," was all I could manage to say.

Sammy looked up at the big wrought-iron clock on the exposed brick wall of the café. "Looks like it's time for me to go. Is there anything you need me to do before I leave?"

I looked around the café. It was mostly empty and fairly clean. Anything that needed to be done, I could take care of easily on my own. "Nope, I think we're good. Enjoy the rest of your day."

She gave me a quick hug then took off her apron and headed out through the back. I grabbed a rag and went to wipe down the tables and straighten up the chairs. An hour later, the café was neat, clean, and in the throes of the late-afternoon lull. There wasn't a single person besides myself in the café. Even Brent Griffin had packed up his laptop and gone after receiving a phone call that left him looking even more annoyed than usual.

I piddled around, straightened up the display cases, and made a few extra mozzarella-tomato-basil sandwiches to have on hand. Eventually I decided to go start working on my first batch of pies. I usually preferred to bake after hours so I wouldn't be interrupted by a customer at any moment, potentially not getting back to what I was doing for a few hours. So much of baking could be time-sensitive that I didn't like to take the risk. But with the café completely empty and my mind constantly drifting back to the theft of the painting, I decided I needed the distraction.

I had just slid the first two pies into the oven when the bell over the door jingled and an elderly man made his way into the café.

"Hello!" I called out. "Welcome to Antonia's Italian Café."

"Hello," he replied warmly. He walked slowly towards the counter, looking around and taking in the café. He smiled at me when he reached the counter. "You know, I believe I was in here a time or two many years ago."

"Really? How long ago?" I loved meeting people who might have known, or at least met, my grandparents.

"Oh, it was probably sixty-some years ago now. This place was new back then. A young couple ran it. They'd just come over from Italy, if I remember correctly. It's been a few years now though, so I might be wrong."

"Those were my grandparents!"

The man's already-pleasant face broke into a full grin. "Still in the family. Imagine that! You don't see that nowadays."

"It's rare, but there are a few shops in Cape Bay that have been passed down through families."

"I'll have to have a walk around and see if I remember anything else. I spent quite a lot of time in here though." He looked around the room again as if seeing it through younger eyes.

"Well, welcome back. I'm thrilled to have you here. Is there anything I can get you, or do you just want to have a look around?"

A grin spread across his face again. "The best cup of coffee I've ever had was in this café. If what you serve is anything like what your grandfather used to make, I'd love a cup of coffee."

"He had a gift for making a great cup of coffee, but I'll see what I can do. Do you want plain coffee? Black? Or do you take it with cream or sugar?"

"You know, your grandfather recommended an americano over regular coffee, and I've been ordering my coffee that way ever since. I'll have one of those, please, young lady. It'll be like old times again."

"One americano, coming up!" I started moving to get a cup and saucer. "If you'd like to take a seat, I'll bring it over to you in just a minute. And don't even think about paying for it."

"If you give away your coffee, you won't have a café to pass down to your own children someday!"

"Long-time customers get special privileges. I'd say you count as long time," I said with a wink.

He looked like he wanted to protest some more, but he just nodded and made his way to one of the tables. As I made his coffee, he gazed around the café with a decidedly dreamy look in his eyes. I imagined he must have had fond memories of the place.

When his coffee was ready and as good as I could make it, I carried it over to him. "Here you go! Is there anything else I can get you?"

"No, thank you. This will be just fine."

"Great! Well, I'll just be over there behind the counter if you change your mind."

"Actually, why don't you sit down here across from me and talk to me for a while. It's not often I get to chat with pretty young ladies anymore."

I didn't have anything else pressing to do and the oven was on a timer, so I figured I had no reason not to sit and talk to him for a while. Besides, what was the point in owning a coffee shop if you didn't get to spend time getting to know new and interesting people? I pulled out the chair and sat down. "I'd be honored, Mister...?"

"Please, call me John."

"It's a pleasure to meet you, John. I'm Fran. Francesca."

"Francesca," he repeated. "Such a lovely name. Italian, isn't it?"

I nodded. "It was my great-grandmother's name."

"Lovely."

I waited while he took a sip of his coffee. I was surprised to find that I was nervous to see his reaction to it. If my grandfather's coffee was the best he'd ever had, I didn't want to let him down with my replica.

"Delicious. Just as good as I remember." He smiled at me. "Now, Francesca, tell me something—didn't I see you at the Louis Cliffton show at the museum last night?"

I realized he must have been the man I saw sitting alone in the museum lobby when Matt and I arrived at the show the night before. I felt a little fluttering of butterflies in my stomach. If he had been at the show, he had seen the portrait! I could talk to him about it. I smiled. "Yes, John, I was."

Chapter Eight

John surprised me with his knowledge of art as we sat at the table and discussed the Cliffton show. Whereas almost everyone who had seen the show or heard about the paintings seemed most focused on the stunning use of gold and jewels, John talked about the way they were used and the feelings they evoked.

He talked about the way the viewer's eye was drawn across the canvas and the way Cliffton manipulated that through his use of the paint and precious materials. He even made several observations about Cliffton's choice to recreate other artists' famous works and then layer his original work on top.

"If you're familiar enough with the original paintings," he said, "you notice that his versions are deliberately not quite right. In the *Water Lilies* painting, *Glimmer No. 5*, I believe he titled it, you'll notice that the colors aren't right. He reversed the pinks and greens. In the *American Gothic* painting–" Here he closed his eyes and rubbed his fingertips together. "*Glimmer No. 3*–the woman is on the man's left instead of his right. It's a subtle way of subverting the established works before he even adds his treatment."

I was torn between asking how on earth he was able to talk about the show on this level and asking what he thought of the stolen painting. I decided on one of my PR techniques for dealing with famous clients and ones who just thought they were–fawn over them. "You have such interesting thoughts on the show. How do you know so much about art?"

He smiled and leaned back a little in his chair. "Fifty years as an art professor makes you quite verbose about painting techniques and quite boring at cocktail parties."

I had to let that roll around in my head for a few seconds. "You've been an art professor for fifty years?"

"I *was* one for fifty years. Now I'm just an old man who goes to museums to look at new art and then bores pretty ladies in quaint cafés with his arcane knowledge."

"You're not boring me at all!" I protested. He really wasn't. I could have sat there and listened to him go on about the paintings for hours. It was only my desire to hear what he thought about the stolen painting that made me anxious to move on from his general observations.

"You needn't flatter me, Francesca. I know I'm just prattling on about things that only interest me."

"No, really! Really!" I repeated it because he didn't look like he believed me. "I was actually wondering what you thought of one of the paintings in particular."

"Really?"

"Yes, really!"

"Which one?" He looked intensely interested, even leaning in towards me.

I wondered how long it had been since he'd retired or, even more than that, since he'd had a genuinely interested audience. I made a mental note to find out how long he was going to be in town if he was, in fact, only visiting—I didn't actually know that yet. If he'd be around for even a few days, I thought he and Sammy might like to talk. She'd probably be fascinated by his insights.

"Did you see the one, kind of in the back, that was based on the *Mona Lisa*?"

He looked faintly surprised then nodded. "I did."

"What did you think of it?"

He took a deep breath and exhaled it slowly then sipped from his cup of coffee. He leaned back in his chair. "It was—" He paused for a long time. So long, in fact, that I first thought he was trying to find a polite way to say that he hated it, and then that perhaps he'd forgotten what I'd asked. "Stunning," he finally said, just when I started thinking that I might need to repeat the question.

I smiled. I had been so afraid that he was going to say that it was terrible that I was genuinely relieved that he approved of it.

"You liked it, I take it?" he said.

I nodded. "It was striking, I thought. And—" I hesitated. I knew what I wanted to say, but John was so much more knowl-edgeable about art than I was that I reluctant to tell him my opinion in case I was wrong.

"And?" he prompted. When I still didn't finish my thought, he smiled gently. "There are no wrong feelings in art. Whatever impression a painting gives you is valid. Art speaks to us all differently."

"Sad," I blurted. "It felt sad."

His eyes stared into mine like they were seeing inside of me. I almost expected him to say that he knew it reminded me of my mother. Instead, he just nodded.

"Did you see the tear?" he asked. "I stood and listened to several people as they looked at it. Most of them didn't see the tear, did you?"

"Yes." I was both surprised and not that people had missed it. It was almost like an optical illusion—you can stare at it forever and never see the hidden picture, but once you do, you can never *not* see it. The strand of gold that was the tear was so fine that it wasn't hard to believe that people over-looked it, but at the same time, it was such a critical part of the work as a whole that I felt like anyone who didn't see it wasn't seeing the real painting.

"Such an excellent use of the medium. It would actually be difficult to replicate the effect with anything other than the gold. A glaze, maybe, but I don't think it would have the same impact."

I shook my head. The gold made it. "It was his mother, you know."

John looked almost startled. I realized my comment probably didn't make sense in the course of the conversation.

"The woman in the painting—she was his mother. Cliffton's, I mean."

John's composure had returned. He nodded. "Yes, I know."

Of course he did. Retired or not, he was an art professor. He probably had some sort of dossier on Cliffton with all of that information.

"I actually got to talk to him at the show last night. Cliffton, I mean. He saw me looking at the painting and came over to talk to me. He said she died recently. My mother did too. I wonder if that's why I saw the tear. And why the painting felt so sad to me."

John was very still for a moment before he nodded. When he spoke, his voice was soft. "We connect with things—paintings, television shows, literature–when we recognize something of ourselves in them." He looked down at the table and then at me. "I'm sorry to hear about your mother. That's quite a loss."

Suddenly I was fighting back tears. "Thank you," I said softly. As I stared at the table, I felt him stuff a napkin in my hand. I looked up at him and smiled before dabbing it under my eyes.

"Thank you. It's been hitting me hard the past couple of days. Since I saw that painting really." My heart clutched as I remembered that it was gone. "Did you hear that it was stolen?" I didn't even wait to give him the chance to say anything. "My friend Sammy– she works here too–she said she wondered if it was stolen just for the gold and jewels. Like the person wanted to scrape them off and sell them. What if she's right? What if whoever took it destroys it?"

John looked as horrified by the idea as I felt. "No, I–I don't think–surely–" He struggled to put his words together.

"But even if they don't–you're an art professor, you probably know about these things–even if they don't destroy the painting to get at the gold and jewels Cliffton used, what are the chances the painting is found? Are art thefts usually solved?"

"Some are," he said slowly. "Many aren't. The people who do these things—sometimes they're opportunists who think they see a way to make a quick fortune. Often though, they're people who have connections in the art world that they know they'll be able to use to get rid of the painting. There's always someone—some Russian oligarch, some Saudi prince, some young fellow with more money than sense—who's willing to buy. It's a pity, really. Who can they ever show it to? Who can they trust? Some of the paintings that are stolen are world-famous, instantly recognizable to even schoolchildren. If you have a painting like that, you can't ever let anyone know you have it. That's why so many stolen paintings are damaged when they're recovered—they end up being hidden in a basement or an attic somewhere so that no one can accidentally see them. But does that account for most stolen paintings? No, I don't think so. Most paintings aren't Munch's *The Scream*. Most paintings can hide in plain sight. And that's why they're so hard to find."

I stared at him for several long seconds. I wasn't sure whether or not to feel comforted by what he said. I didn't think the Cliffton painting, despite being reminiscent of the *Mona Lisa*, quite counted as the kind of world-famous, instantly recognizable masterpiece that had to be hidden in a barn to keep from being discovered. The gems scattered across it certainly made it more distinctive than your average, run-of-the-mill, museum-quality painting, but its distinctiveness hadn't stopped the thief from taking it.

I thought over the possibilities. It could have been taken so that the thief could, in essence, sell it for scrap. It could have been taken by someone just hoping to sell it and make a quick buck, with no particular potential buyer in mind. Or it could have been taken by someone with the kind of connections that would make it disappear forever. I didn't like any of those choices.

Before I could think about it any further, my oven timer went off.

"Excuse me, John, I need to go take my pies out of the oven. I'll be right back."

"I was wondering what that delicious smell was. Apple, if I'm not mistaken?"

"That's right!" I called back to him. I slid the two pies out of the oven and laid them out to cool. Once they had cooled down sufficiently that they wouldn't feel like molten lava in your mouth, I'd offer him a slice. It would be a nice treat for my new friend who was an old friend of Antonia's. I put the other two pies I'd prepared into the oven and set the timer again.

As I headed back to the table, I recognized an uncomfortable feeling creeping up in my chest. It was an anxiousness, an itch of sorts. No matter how little I wanted to indulge it, I knew I wouldn't be able to fight it off. But no matter how much I didn't like that feeling, I knew Mike would like it even less.

I couldn't let the painting stay missing. Despite my every intention to the contrary, I wasn't going to stay out of it. I had to do whatever I could to make sure it was found. I was getting involved.

Chapter Nine

I was cuddled up on the couch with Matt, Latte sprawled across our legs like it was the only logical place for him to be. Every time one of us moved, he adjusted himself to get more comfortable. If either of us got up, Latte waited patiently until we returned then wiggled himself back into place. At least he was warm. The temperature outside was in the low thirties, and Matt's old house was poorly insulated. Despite the heater running and the fireplace roaring, it was still a bit nippy. I was grateful for the warmth of Matt, Latte, and the americano I clutched in my hands.

"Why is it called that again?" Matt asked, taking a sip from his own drink.

"An americano?"

"Yeah. Why's it called an 'American' but the word is in Italian?"

I chuckled. "You want me to play coffee historian for you?"

Matt looked at me with his eyes squinted. "That depends on how long of a speech it's going to be." He glanced sideways at the TV that predictably was showing a football game.

I laughed again. "I'll be brief."

"Have at it then."

"So, actual coffee historians are split on it, but my grandfather said that back during World War II, when the Americans who were deployed to Italy came into his family's café, he noticed that they would add extra water to their espresso to make it more like the coffee they had back home. Once he caught on, he started asking them if they wanted him to go ahead and add the water—that way it would at least be clean, hot water instead of whatever they were carrying around in their canteens, you know? His family started calling it *caffè americano* among themselves, and then the GIs picked it up and just started ordering it that way. He figured that was happening at cafés everywhere the Allies were camped, and then it spread as they made their way up to Rome and then through Northern Italy."

"So your grandfather didn't take all the credit for it—just some of it." Matt grinned.

I swatted at him, momentarily drawing Latte's interest. When he decided that nothing was going on that involved food or his comfortable sleeping position, he laid his head down and went back to sleep.

"My grandfather wasn't taking credit for it. He was just saying that that's how it happened in his little neck of the woods."

"I know, I'm just teasing." Matt slid his arms around me, jostling Latte again, and kissed me. It was very romantic until Latte stood up on my lap and started "kissing" our faces. Matt leaned back on the couch, laughing. I wiped the dog drool from my face with the sleeve of Matt's sweatshirt that I was borrowing.

"I don't think I ever asked you how your day went," he said after staring at the football game for a few minutes in which all I could tell that was accomplished was the guys rearranging themselves on the field.

"It was pretty good. It got a little busy a couple times, but it was slow and steady most of the day. Sammy and Becky loved the apple pie, and I got six made and ready to sell tomorrow. I have two more prepped so that Sammy can just pop them in the oven to sell by the slice." I paused for a second and tilted my head to look up at him from where I had my head rested on his shoulder. His eyes were on the TV, but he raised his eyebrows expectantly, like he was waiting for whatever I had to say. "Did you know that my mom always sold apple pies in the café this time of year?"

Matt's eyes got rounder, and he pursed his lips like he was trying to figure out how to answer the question. "Umm..."

"Matty," I said, my tone warning him that I knew he was stalling.

"It sounds familiar."

"Familiar like, yes, of course, everybody in town knew and nobody wanted to tell me?"

"Well, I wouldn't say it like that exactly."

"How would you say it then?"

"More like, yes, I knew, but I thought it might be too painful for you to make your mom's signature pie, so I didn't want to say anything." He looked down at me with his best puppy-dog eyes. I could see the tenderness and compassion in them.

"You're sweet," I said and ran my fingers through his hair.

I knew exactly what he meant. His dad had been the town barber and was the only person to cut Matt's hair his entire life until he passed away over the summer. Matt had gotten his hair cut once or twice since then, but he was definitely due for another cut. His hair was getting borderline shaggy, but I'd avoided saying anything for fear of causing him any kind of pain. Besides, he had eyes and a mirror. He knew he needed a trim. I, on the other hand, hadn't known about my mom's annual pie sales. But then again, Sammy thought I knew about my mom's pies. I twirled a lock of Matt's rich-brown hair around my finger.

"Yeah, I know it's getting long," he said, as if reading my thoughts.

"Sorry, I wasn't trying to hint—" I stopped and dropped my hand to his neck.

"I didn't say you should stop!" He tipped his head back and tried to rub it across my hand. I took the less-than-subtle hint and started playing with his hair again.

He watched the football game for a minute while I ran my fingers through his hair. "It's just weird having someone other than my dad do it, you know? It doesn't feel like I should be letting a stranger touch my head."

"Don't you know the guy who bought out your dad's shop?"

"Yeah, but–" He shrugged. "I'd feel like I was cheating on Dad. I already feel like I'm cheating on Dad. But in his shop with another barber? Couldn't do it."

I smiled as I wrapped his hair around my fingers. If it was going to be longish, at least it was soft and fun to play with.

The football game cut to the billionth or so commercial break, and a teaser for the eleven o'clock news came on.

"Tonight's top story: a million-dollar art heist in a local vacation spot. We'll have the latest developments, live at eleven!" an enthusiastic anchorwoman said over muted footage of Mike talking to the camera before the sports and weather guys each did their five-second promos.

"Did you hear about that?" I asked.

Matt nodded. "Big news. Couple of guys from work texted me to see if I had any inside information since they know I live in town."

"Do you?" I figured he would have told me if he did, but we hadn't discussed the theft, so maybe he just hadn't mentioned it yet.

He laughed. "Nope, but I wouldn't be surprised if you do."

"What? Why?"

"Because you're Francesca Amaro, amateur sleuth extraordinaire."

I rolled my eyes. "It's not like I go sticking my nose in every crime in Cape Bay."

"You mean all our graffiti and the money stolen out of unlocked cars? Those are beneath you," he teased. "You save your skills for felonies."

At best, Matt only borderline approved of my investigations, so it seemed strange that he was joking about me getting involved in this one. I leaned over and sniffed his coffee.

"What are you doing?" He pulled it away from me.

"Did you slip some whiskey in there? You don't usually joke about my investigations."

"That's because you're usually involved in one when we talk about them." He lifted his mug to take another sip of his coffee but stopped with it halfway to his mouth. "Oh, no, you're not getting involved in this one, are you?"

I shrugged and kept playing with his hair nonchalantly. It wasn't like I'd done anything to really get involved yet.

"Franny?"

"Of all the paintings, they took my favorite one. And from all the way in the back too! Why that one? Why not take one of the ones up front?"

"Didn't the one you liked have more of the stuff on it than the others?"

"The gold and gems? Yes, but—"

"Maybe they took that one because it was the biggest bang for the buck. One painting, several hundred thousand dollars' worth of materials. To get that much from the others, you'd have to take a few of them."

"You think they just took it for the metal and jewels?" My heart sank. It was my greatest fear about the robbery. The idea that someone would take that stunning painting just to destroy it—it made me want to do anything I could to get it back as quickly as possible.

"Not a lot of art connoisseurs in Cape Bay."

"That's what Sammy thought too—that it was stolen for the materials. John didn't seem to think so, but—"

"John?" Matt interrupted.

"Oh, he's this sweet older man I met at Antonia's today. He was an art professor in Boston for fifty years. And apparently, he came to the café a few times back right after my grandparents opened it. He remembered talking to my grandfather and everything. *And* apparently, my grandfather recommended an americano to him, and he's been ordering them ever since!"

"Smart man." Matt gave a mock toasting gesture with his mug and drank from it. "So you talked to this John about the painting?"

I nodded. "He was at the show last night, so he'd seen it. Do you remember when we first walked in and there was an older man sitting in the lobby?"

Matt wrinkled his forehead and looked unsure.

"Anyway, that was him. We talked about art for quite a while this afternoon. It was lovely."

Matt nodded as he watched the football players on the TV slam into each other and land in a pile on the turf. "Yes!" He pumped his fist. I had no idea which team he was cheering for or what they'd done to earn his approval. The game cut to another break. "So, you want to figure out who took the painting, huh?"

I nodded, somewhat hesitantly.

He sighed. "What are your theories so far?"

"I don't really know. I haven't had much of a chance to think about it yet. From what John and I discussed, I guess there are two possibilities—someone took it for the materials or to sell to some shady collector."

Matt nodded thoughtfully. "Or to keep for themselves."

I thought about it for a second. "But who that was there would have done that? The only people who saw it and knew it was there were the people at the opening, and it was all locals there last night. Who in Cape Bay would steal a painting like that? What would they do with it? They couldn't exactly put it up on their wall. Anyone in town would recognize it if they saw it."

"I didn't recognize those security guards."

"You think one of the security guards took it just so he could look at it whenever he wanted?"

Matt shrugged. "Never know. One of them might have been an art history major. Not a lot of other jobs you can get with that degree." He smirked. I rolled my eyes.

"I don't know. I feel like the financial aspect is more likely. Like you said, it was the most expensive painting in there."

"I am a very smart man," he deadpanned. I rolled my eyes again, but I couldn't help smiling. The twinkle in his eye was very cute.

"Of course you are." I trailed my fingers from his hair down to his neck. His eyes closed as he rolled his head forward to give me better access. Afraid of losing his attention if I kept up, I rested my hand on his shoulder. "So, Mr. Smart Man, who are our suspects?"

Matt shrugged. "You're the investigator, not me. Who had the most to gain financially?"

I thought about it and came up pretty much empty. "Whoever could sell it for the best price?"

Matt chuckled. "Well, yeah."

It wasn't an easy question. Whoever had the most to gain was whoever could sell it for the best price. Or, I realized, whoever thought they could. It wasn't like an auction where they bid on it. So it was either someone with the knowledge and connections to find a buyer who could afford it and was willing to buy it on the black market, or it was someone who thought they could make a quick buck and for whom that money would be a big deal, even if they didn't manage to get what the painting was actually worth.

I thought about those security guards. Matt was right—neither of them looked familiar. I would have expected Mike to hire off-duty cops or even some of the temporary guys who worked during the tourist season. I wondered where Mike had found them. And it was suspicious that the thief—or thieves—had managed to get the painting at all if the security was as good as Sammy told me Ryan said it would be. Who would know how to get around it like the security guards?

I rested my head back on Matt's shoulder and slipped my arm through his. He laid his hand on my leg just above my knee. Latte wiggled to adjust to our new positions. That dog could sleep like none other. I watched the football players move around on the screen without even trying to figure out what was going on. My mind was still on the painting.

When another commercial for the news came on, this one with the cheery anchor-woman's disembodied voice asking, "Who is Louis Cliffton? Everything you need to know about the local artist coming up at eleven!" I felt a thought creep into the back of my mind. Not wanting to entertain it, I quickly banished it. Thoughts aren't good listeners though, so it kept creeping back until I couldn't ignore it anymore.

"Matty?" I rubbed his leg with my thumb.

"Hmm?"

"You don't think—never mind." Apparently, my tongue was more accepting of my desire to push the thought out of my mind than my mind itself had been.

"What?" Matt asked, prompting me to say it.

"What if Cliffton took the painting himself?" The words came out of my mouth so softly even I could barely hear them.

From Matt's stillness, I could tell the thought made sense to him. "He'd get the insurance money, wouldn't he?"

I nodded against his shoulder. "And a lot of publicity. Do you think those guys at your office had heard of Cliffton before today?"

Matt scoffed. "I hadn't heard of him until you told me about his show at the museum."

"Oh, and if you've never heard of him, no one has?" I teased. I wiggled my fingers against his abdomen, and he pulled away, laughing. Latte huffed as he readjusted himself across our legs.

Matt reached over to the end table and grabbed his phone. He tapped at it one-handed then, holding it out in front of him, began reading.

"What's this about a painting getting stolen in Cape Bay? Is Cliffton a big deal around there or something?" He tapped some more and read again. "I'd never heard of that Cliffton guy until you mentioned him the other day, and now he's all over the news. Apparently, people other than me know who he is." Matt tapped again and looked over at me. "More?"

"No, I believe you."

He put his phone down and resumed his previous position. I snuggled back in. Latte wiggled himself comfortable.

As much as I hated to admit it, it seemed like Cliffton had at least two good reasons to steal the painting himself–money and fame. I'd learned over my thirty-four, almost-thirty-five years, especially the ten spent in public relations, that people would do a lot of stupid, crazy things for money and fame. And for a lot of them, it didn't even have to be real fame–notoriety worked just as well. Of course, the security guards had better access to the painting than anyone else and could stand to make a pretty penny on the painting's materials alone. But these were just ideas–I was nowhere near close to having an idea of who the thief might be yet. I had a lot of people to talk to and a lot of questions to ask.

My late night the night before was catching up to me. The warmth from the fire and the dog and the man had finally reached my bones, and despite the many cups of coffee I'd had during the day, including the one I'd just finished, my eyes were getting heavy. The football game didn't look like it was going to be over anytime soon, so I thought I'd take a quick nap.

Just as my eyes closed, I realized there was someone else who stood to gain a good bit of publicity from the theft—the museum owner, Adam Shuster.

Chapter Ten

As I walked into the café late the next morning, I was greeted by the warm, spicy smell of apple pie.

"Your pies are a hit, Fran!" Sammy called as soon as she spotted me.

"They are? Already?" I slipped my apron on over my head and pulled the strings around behind my back to tie it.

She nodded from the counter and waved a piece of paper in the air. "There's a wait list."

I stopped in my tracks. "There is? Are you serious?"

She laughed her pretty Sammy laugh. "Uh-huh! It started slow this morning, but as soon as word got out, they were sold."

She paused for a second. "Well, most of them were sold. I had to snag one of them so that we had some to sell by the slice. Oh, and I hope you don't mind—I asked Rhonda if she could run by the grocery store and pick up some vanilla ice cream for us so we can serve the pie à la mode."

I was still staring at her with my apron half-tied. "It's eleven thirty."

"Uh-huh."

"And you've sold five pies."

"Well, six and a half, if you count the slices."

"At eleven thirty in the morning."

She giggled. "Uh-huh."

I managed to regain my senses enough to finish tying my apron. "How is that possible?"

"People love your mom's pie that much. They're excited to see it back."

I was still struggling to wrap my mind around it. "But who's buying pie first thing in the morning?"

Sammy shrugged. "Some people still have big Sunday dinners. They come in for a cup of coffee, see that we have pies, and figure they have dessert taken care of. Plus,

St. Catherine's has a potluck after mass every week—I think at least one of the pies was headed over there."

"How many names are on the wait list?"

"Five."

"Another five?"

"Well, names. It's—" She paused as she tapped her finger on the paper and counted silently. "Nine pies. Two ones, two twos, and a three."

"Nine?" I was shocked. Nine pies. I had no idea Cape Bay liked pie that much. Then something occurred to me. "They're not all for tomorrow, are they?"

Sammy nodded solemnly before breaking into a grin. "No, I didn't know how many you wanted to make each day, so I told the last two people that we'd already presold everything for Monday and they'd have to wait until Tuesday."

I breathed a sigh of relief. Nine preordered pies plus three or four to sell by the slice would be a lot of pies to make in a day. I could do it as long as the café wasn't too busy or I had someone to take care of customers while I baked.

The only real problem was that I had hoped to spend at least some of the day finding out whatever I could about my potential suspects in the art theft. I was actually even hoping that Cliffton's assistant, Brent, might come in again. He obviously spent a lot of time with Cliffton and presumably knew some of his idiosyncrasies—like whether he worried about money or his reputation. Brent also probably would have been closely involved in the setup of the exhibit and would know about the security—including whether the hired guards had seemed a little too interested in the art as it was going up. I'd still have to make eight pies, but that was easier than twelve.

"That sounds good," I said. "Thank you."

"Of course." Sammy smiled slyly as she picked up another piece of paper from the counter. "That doesn't include the Thanksgiving orders."

I glanced at the list. It was longer than the wait list. I didn't want to think about how much longer. I wanted to change the subject. "So, you said you asked Rhonda to pick up some ice cream?"

"Yup. I figure it'll be a hit. And if it's not, we can eat it ourselves." Sammy grinned.

"People have actually already been asking about it."

"It's eleven thirty!" It was the third time I'd said it, but I honestly couldn't get over it. I didn't know people thought about pie this openly this early in the morning. Sure, at home, if there was pie, I might sneak a piece for breakfast, but I always thought that was sort of something to be ashamed of. Apparently, not in Cape Bay.

A customer came in and approached the counter. Sammy went over to take care of him, giving me a chance to survey the café. It was moderately full, about what I expected for late on a Sunday morning. It was mostly individuals, with a few small groups—couples, friends meeting up, a couple of young guys who looked like they were nursing hangovers.

We didn't serve brunch per se, but we had salads and sandwiches that people liked. In a little less than an hour, we'd get a small rush of families stopping in on their way home from mass at St. Catherine's or else from the Presbyterian church on the other side of town. I'd thought about adding some hot food to the menu for them and the brunchers, but after the pumpkin spice screwup, I figured I needed to wait until I got my footing in the café a little more.

I headed around the corner to go check on the customers and clear any tables I could. As I passed Sammy, she shot a meaningful glance at the apple pie she was plating for the customer who had just come in. People really did eat pie in the morning.

I smiled and chatted to the customers as I made my way around the room, greeting the ones I knew by name and being pleasantly sociable to the ones I didn't. When I got to the back corner, I was pleasantly surprised to see Brent Griffin holed up with his laptop, again wearing his tweed professor jacket. I had a feeling he wore that a lot.

"Brent!" I said as cheerily as I could. "It's great to see you! Working on your novel?"

For a few seconds, he just stared at me like he wasn't sure who I was or where I'd appeared from. Then finally, he smiled, pulled off his glasses, and leaned back in his chair. "Ah, Francesca, isn't it?"

I smiled warmly and nodded. "It's great to see you back again. I guess you're finding the café a good place to write?"

"I am. I am. The energy of the people here, the locals, it's very inspiring. I often write in cafés in the city—New York, I mean—so I'm used to blocking out the hustle and bustle, but here, the energy's different. The people are so—simple. I hope to capture that spirit to use for some of the less sophisticated, more salt-of-the-earth characters in my novel."

I tried to keep the smile plastered on my face and pretend that what he said wasn't insulting. Calling him out would do nothing to help me get information from him. And maybe he'd be more open to talking if he thought I was some backwards yokel. "That's so impressive—that you can just take people you see and work them into your book," I said, playing up my Massachusetts accent.

"My *novel*," he corrected. I tried not to visibly react. "And, yes, it's the gift—the duty, really—of the writer to bring the life he sees around him into vivid detail on the page. If I couldn't find inspiration in the people I see around me, my characters would be hollow husks."

Hollow husks. I wondered if his whole book was filled with similarly alliterative redundancies. "You know, if you need a break, now or later, I'd love to talk to you more about your b—your novel, I mean. And your process. Artists fascinate me. If you'd be willing to, of course." I smiled and tried to look like I was somewhat starstruck by his talent.

"Of course!" He looked even more eager than I'd expected. "I actually just finished a particularly intense scene, so I could use a bit of a break. And perhaps another cup of coffee?"

"Absolutely. And would you like a piece of warm apple pie? It's an old family recipe." I figured playing up the "salt of the earth" angle would entice him, if nothing else.

He twitched one eyebrow up. "Yes, I'd like that."

"I'll be right back." I grabbed his empty cup and hurried back behind the counter. "Sammy, could you get me a couple pieces of pie, please? And what was Brent drinking?"

"The artist's assistant?" she asked.

I nodded as I grabbed a couple of cups and saucers. You better believe I was going to sit there and make myself comfortable while he talked. Whatever I could do to make him feel like chatting.

"A nonfat sugar-free soy mocha pumpkin spice latte with an extra shot of espresso, extra cinnamon, and extra whipped cream. And some cinnamon sprinkled on top of the whipped cream."

I stopped my hurrying. "What? Does that even make sense?"

"Not really, but he was insistent, and he seemed happy with what I made him."

"Oookay," I said, drawing out the word into multiple syllables.

I made my best approximation of his drink and then fixed myself a quick americano. His excessively elaborate pumpkin spice latte had taken so long that I didn't even want to take the time to make myself a latte for fear that he'd get tired of waiting and go back to writing his novel, making me lose my chance to talk to him.

Sammy helped me carry the drinks and pie back to Brent's table, and I sat down across from him.

Brent picked up the pie plate and waved it under his nose with his eyes closed, inhaling deeply like he was sniffing wine. "Mmm, apples, cinnamon. And do I detect nutmeg?" He put the plate back down without so much as glancing my way for an answer. Then he picked up his coffee cup and repeated the routine. Instead of putting it down, though, he took a sip and swished it around his mouth, eyes again closed. I watched him, both because I wanted to see what he thought of it and because I fully expected him to spit it out since he seemed to think he was at a wine tasting.

Thankfully, he swallowed it. He picked up his fork and took the smallest sliver of apple pie from the plate to his mouth. He didn't swish it, probably because it's difficult to swish solid food, but he did seem to roll it around with his tongue before swallowing. I took a normal bite of my pie and a normal sip of my coffee.

"So, tell me more about your novel," I said when he finally seemed finished with his performance. "You said it was an epic?"

"Indeed," he replied and launched into a detailed description of the plot, the characters, the setting, how the setting was really a character in the novel, how the structure of the novel mirrored the structure of the central family, and on and on and on and on. I tried to keep up and ask relevant questions, but the whole thing seemed excessively convoluted. I hoped for his sake that the book made more sense than his explanation of it.

I kept trying to find an opportunity to bring up Cliffton and the painting, but even aside from the fact that I could barely get a word in, I didn't really see a chance to bring it up naturally. Finally though, he started talking about how much he'd written and how much he had left to write.

"It's just over three hundred pages now, and I'm about a third of the way through, so that's another six hundred pages. Ultimately, after the editing process, I hope to come in around seven hundred and fifty pages. A bit long for a first novel, but, as I believe I mentioned, it's an epic."

"Wow!" I was more excited to finally see my opening than about how long his book was going to be. "And you've written all that while working full time for Louis Cliffton? That's really impressive!"

"Thank you, Francesca. Unfortunately, Cliffton doesn't see it that way. He spends all his time on his art, leaving me no time to pursue my own. My days are completely taken up by dealing with his humdrum administrative nonsense."

I bit my tongue to keep from making a comment about that being pretty much the definition of an assistant's job. Instead, I played dumb and asked Brent about the humdrum administrative nonsense. "Is there a lot of administrative work that needs to be done for an artist?"

"There is actually. All his financials, his fan mail, his gallery shows and sales, he makes me handle all of that. I don't think he's spoken to a single gallery owner since I started working for him. The current show down at the little 'museum'"–he punctuated the word with air quotes and a disgusted look on his face–"I had to coordinate all of that. All Cliffton said was that he wanted to have a show in this little town and I had to handle the rest. He mentioned the museum, but did he want to contact the owner or deal with the complete lack of security? No, that was all me."

"Oh, you handled the security?"

Brent snorted. "I coordinated it. That museum owner–that Shuster–and some local cop did the legwork. I just approved what they designed."

I saw an opening to ask him about something I hadn't anticipated. While playing dumb, of course. "So the security was good? Because, you know..." I let my voice trail off.

"Of course it was good!" he snapped. "I wouldn't have approved it if it wasn't!"

"Oh, no no no, I know! I wasn't trying to say that what you approved wasn't good–just that, well, you saw the museum. It's not exactly world-class." I was a little taken aback by his outburst and was doing my best to get the conversation back on track.

He snorted again. "Indeed. By the contract, the museum owner is supposed to pay for all of that. But he couldn't cover it all, so the remainder had to be paid with Cliffton's funds. With the value of those paintings, we couldn't have subpar security."

"I can imagine. And you handle all his finances too?"

Brent nodded. "He has no talent for anything but art. If I didn't handle the books for him, he wouldn't know if he had a hundred dollars or a hundred million. Well, he still doesn't, but at least somebody does."

"That somebody being you." I tried to sound impressed.

Brent nodded again. "I know every penny that goes in or out of his accounts."

"It sounds like there's a lot of pressure on you, handling all of those things and making all of those decisions."

"There is. And for all my trouble, Cliffton pays me scarcely enough to afford rent, let alone enough to dress and feed myself." He ran his fingers over his lapel. "Gucci doesn't come cheap, you know."

I was pretty sure Gucci didn't make tweed jackets, but again, I bit my tongue. Making a smart comment would get me nowhere. Instead, I took the other opening I saw. "Oh, is money a problem for him?" Something flared in Brent's eyes, and I hurried to make it about him. "Since he's paying you so poorly and all?"

"If it was, I might excuse it. But Cliffton is swimming in cash. He has family money to start with—he was a trust-fund baby and inherited millions when his father died—and his paintings are selling for millions more."

Another opening. I acted surprised. "Really? He doesn't seem very well known for someone whose paintings are selling for that much."

Brent chuckled. "I can see how you'd think that, living somewhere so provincial—"

My tongue had gotten sore, so I bit the inside of my lower lip this time.

"–but Clifton is a star of the art world. He's invited to a party or gala every night of the week, not that he even wants to go. He'd rather stay home and work on his art or moon over his dead mother."

Was that blood I tasted? I was certainly biting my lip hard enough.

Brent, oblivious, kept talking as he tended to do. "He may not be a household name in Middle America, but why would he need to be? Those people can't afford his paintings. They probably don't even understand them. No, Clifton has all the fame he needs or wants. Now, that actually reminds me of the plight of one of my characters. You know Zeke, Amandala's son? His character arc–"

While Brent expounded on the minutiae of his characters' lives, I thought about what he'd just told me. Clifton didn't need the insurance money from the painting, nor did he need the fame. He was basically out as a suspect. I was relieved. He'd been so nice at the museum that I hadn't wanted to think he could have stolen the painting.

Brent had, however, inadvertently given me a new suspect: himself.

Chapter Eleven

I finally managed to extricate myself from Brent after about the fifth time I said that I didn't want to take up any more of his novel-writing time. Even then, it was none of my doing that got me away. It was all Mike.

He came into the café, looking for his afternoon coffee fix, and immediately saw me sitting in the corner with Brent. From the look on his face, I guessed he wasn't too thrilled about it. Of course, by that point, neither was I. I was more than happy for Mike to interrupt, even if it meant being on the receiving end of a lecture on staying out of police investigations.

"Hello, Mr. Griffin," Mike said, striding up to the table.

"Officer Stanton." Brent, on the other hand, looked significantly less than thrilled to see Mike. I wondered if they'd had a run-in or if Brent just wasn't happy about the painting being stolen despite Mike's security.

"*Detective* Stanton," Mike growled. It sounded like there was no love lost between either of them.

"Detective Stanton," Brent repeated, sounding less than impressed.

Mike eyed Brent for another few seconds before turning to me. "Francesca, I see you've met Mr. Griffin here."

I knew I was in trouble when he used my full name. I didn't care though. "I have," I said cheerily. "Brent has been telling me about his novel!"

He looked from me to Brent and back again to me. "I see. And is that all?" Before I could answer, he looked over at Brent. "Fran here can have a tendency to be a little curious."

"You make it sound like that's a bad thing!" Sensing that Mike was about to walk away and leave me alone again with Brent and his ego, I glanced behind Mike over towards the counter. "Oh! It looks like

Sammy could use a hand." I stood up and grabbed our dirty dishes. "Great talking to you, Brent. Stay as long as you like. Come back any time! Let us know if you need a refill." I realized I sounded a little maniacal, but I was desperate to get away from Brent's endless monologue about his book. And besides, I wanted to grab Mike before he left to ask him a few questions about the security setup and guards.

I made a beeline for the back room and dropped off the dishes before heading back out to the front counter. Sammy already had Mike's coffee prepared and sitting on the counter waiting for him. She gave me a funny look as I picked it up just before he could. I wouldn't describe the look he gave me as funny though. Annoyed would be more accurate.

"May I have my coffee, please, Fran?" He sounded tired.

"Actually, I was hoping we could talk for a few minutes."

He tipped his head and gestured with his hand to indicate I should go ahead.

"In the back room?"

He exhaled wearily and motioned for me to go first.

"Door closed, I assume?" he asked once we were safely away from the customers.

"Yes, please."

He closed the door and then just stood there and looked at me.

"I was wondering if I could ask you—"

"Could I have my coffee, please, Fran?"

I'd forgotten I had it. "Oh! Yes! Here." I held it out and he took it, immediately tipping it back and taking a long drink from it. So long, in fact, that I was afraid Sammy had served him lukewarm coffee. I didn't know how anyone could drink that much hot, fresh coffee at once.

"All right, go ahead," he said when he was finally done. His voice sounded hoarse, and his face had an odd tension to it.

"Are you okay?"

"Yeah, just—" He coughed then took a breath and shook his head a little. "Coffee's kind of hot."

"You could have waited a minute for it to cool off."

"I'm tired, Fran. Investigating an art theft is surprisingly tough business."

"Oh, yeah?" I was hoping that if I just offered a sympathetic ear, he would volunteer the information I was looking for.

"Yeah."

For a second, I thought he was about to open up to me, but the caffeine must have hit him because all of a sudden, his gaze on me sharpened.

"So what did you want to talk about?" It didn't quite sound like an accusation, but it didn't quite sound like it wasn't one either.

I tried to figure out what the best approach would be. Mike had known me too long and we were too good of friends for me to play dumb. He had already been suspicious yesterday that I was going to investigate his case, and I knew that him spotting me talking to Brent as soon as he walked into the café today didn't help. There was no way I was going to lie to him, and the fact that I'd pulled him into the back room to talk meant that he knew I was either looking for information or had some to give. It was unavoidable—I was going to have to just come out and say it.

"The art heist."

The corner of Mike's mouth turned up. "Heist?"

"Well, what would you call it?"

"We've been investigating it as felony larceny, but calling it a heist is much more poetic."

"Okay, I want to talk about the felony larceny of the Cliffton painting."

"I can't say I'm surprised. What did you want to discuss?"

I took a deep breath. "The security. And the security guards."

"I personally supervised all of that, Fran. The security was good."

"The painting was stolen."

"Paintings get stolen all the time."

I stared at him. "Brent said that the museum couldn't afford to pay for all of it and Cliffton himself had to partly cover it."

Mike nodded.

"Did that seem suspicious to you? That Adam agreed to host such an important show, but he didn't want to pay for the kind of security it needed?"

"This is my investigation, Fran."

"It was just a question, Mike."

His eyes met mine, and I held them without flinching. I knew it was his investigation and he didn't need my help, but I also suspected his pride was keeping him from admitting to any holes in the security.

Finally, Mike exhaled and looked away. "The security system I recommended was state of the art. That's what they told me they wanted. There was no budget. I didn't ask who paid for what. I told them what they needed, and it's their fault that they didn't get it. Do you think I thought this was a good idea? Million-dollar paintings in Adam Shuster's rinky-dink little museum? I knew who would end up investigating if something disappeared out of that place. I have plenty to do without the state police and the FBI breathing down my collar about some painting going missing. If it was up to me, I'd happily turn it over to them, but the Chief doesn't want to give it up. I don't need to have you on my back about it too. Trust me, Fran, there are enough people on this case that you don't need to get involved. Now is there anything else you wanted to know?"

I actually felt sorry for him. As attached as I was to this case, his reputation and maybe even his career were on the line.

He'd done his best to prevent any of the art from being stolen, and he'd failed. And now even I was looking at him and asking why. I shook my head.

"Then I'm going to get another cup of coffee." He dropped the empty coffee cup that he'd somehow managed to drain into the trash and turned towards the door.

"Wait, did you say they didn't get what you recommended?"

He stopped and turned back around. "They got some of it. But I told them they needed pressure sensors on the hooks the paintings would be hanging from and cameras on each painting, and they didn't get either. I don't know if it was a money thing or if they just didn't think it was necessary."

"What about the security guards? They're not locals, are they?"

"I don't know where they're from. I wanted to use off-duty officers—my guys—but Griffin out there had some private firm he wanted to use. I coordinated the schedule to make sure there was twenty-four-seven coverage, but I don't personally know much about the guys. The company's legit, all their guys are supposed to be licensed and bonded, so there was nothing I could really say about them not wanting to take my advice."

"Do you know whether it was Adam or Brent who decided what security to go with?"

"I don't know. I mostly talked to Griffin. Adam just seemed to be going along with whatever Griffin said."

"Did that seem strange to you? I mean, it's Adam's gallery."

Mike looked at me like he expected better of me.

"Sorry, it's your investigation."

Mike nodded. "Anything else? Or can I go get my coffee now?"

"Just one last thing—when will the museum reopen?"

"It's open today. I think Adam would have lost his mind if we didn't turn the place back over to him today. Griffin too. The two of them—" He stopped and just shook his head then opened the door and walked back out into the café. "Could I get another cup of coffee when you get a chance, Sammy?"

"Sure thing!" I heard Sammy say back.

I followed Mike back out into the café. Sammy handed him his coffee.

"Thanks, Sammy." He looked at me. "And try to stay out of trouble, Franny."

"I'll try."

He just shook his head. He stopped for a few seconds to talk to two men at one of the tables then headed for the door. He waved briefly to Sammy and me and then was gone.

"What was that about?" Sammy asked. "The art heist?"

I nodded. "And thank you for calling it that." I felt more than a little vindicated to hear her use the same phrase I had.

"An art heist? That's what it was, wasn't it?"

"Mike says it's a felony larceny."

"Oh, a heist sounds much more mysterious than a plain old larceny."

"That's what I think. Anyway, yes, that's what we were talking about."

"I thought you were staying out of it." Her blue eyes sparkled mischievously.

"Yeah, I was and then... I wasn't."

"Got too curious?"

I sighed. "That was my favorite painting in the show." I paused and looked at her for a second, debating whether I should say what I was thinking. I decided Sammy wouldn't judge me for being cheesy about art and went for it. "I know it sounds ridiculous, but it spoke to me. I connected with it. The thought that it's gone? That I might never see it again or it might be destroyed? It hurts me. I have to do whatever I can to at least try to help find it."

I probably sounded a little melodramatic, but it was how I actually felt.

"Oh, Franny." Sammy pulled me in for a hug. "It doesn't sound ridiculous at all. I bet Louis Cliffton would be honored to hear you say that."

"Thanks," I said. I glanced over at the two men Mike had spoken to. They looked familiar, but I didn't think they were locals. "Speaking of Cliffton, have you seen him? I invited him to come by the café, but that was before the heist." I emphasized the last word and exchanged a little smile with Sammy.

"I heard he went back to Boston yesterday morning."

"Yesterday morning? Right after the painting was stolen?"

She nodded. "Talked to the police and then left. Somebody"—she nodded in Brent's direction—"isn't too happy about being left to deal with it all."

After hearing him talk about how little he liked being expected to deal with the setup of the museum exhibition, I couldn't say I was surprised. I don't know what he thought an assistant was supposed to do, but he sure didn't seem happy about doing much in the way of assisting.

"Do you know if he was planning to leave Saturday? Or was it just because of the painting?" I asked.

Sammy shrugged. "Not sure, but it sounded like he'd been planning on staying through the whole show."

I thought about that for a second. On the one hand, it seemed strange that he would leave right after the portrait of his recently deceased mother was stolen, but on the other hand, he was just going back up to Boston—it wasn't like he was in California. I supposed that since the show was the only reason he was in town, the museum being closed meant he had no reason to stay. Maybe he didn't expect the police to let the museum reopen so soon. Maybe he was already on his way back. I didn't think he was a suspect, but I still wanted to know why he left. And maybe, if I could get a chance to talk to him, I could find out if he was aware of Brent's disdain for his job.

"Do you know where he was staying?" I asked. People liked to talk to Sammy, so she always had inside information.

"Out at Honey B's."

I should have guessed. Despite its silly name, Honey B's B&B—what its owner, Honey Ballard, actually called it—was the nicest place in town.

"Are you thinking of paying her a visit?" Sammy asked, smiling.

"Do you think she'd have time to talk to me?" I tried to hold back my own smile.

"Oh, I don't know. You know how Honey is," she said with pretend innocence in her voice.

"Always happy to talk to anyone and everyone about anything under the sun?"

Sammy laughed. "Yup, pretty much."

I glanced at the big wrought-iron clock on the wall to see how much time I had left before Sammy went home.

"Oh, just go! I'm not in any rush," Sammy said, reading my mind. "I don't have any plans until dinnertime."

"Ooh, you have dinner plans? With who?" I teased.

"I didn't say I had dinner plans. I said I had plans at dinnertime. Now go before I change my mind!"

"Yes, ma'am!" I pulled my apron off and went into the back room for my jacket and handbag. I had done basically nothing useful in the time I'd been at the café, but I knew I'd be there late, probably well after closing time, in order to get the apple pies ready for the next day, so I didn't feel too bad about it. Still, I knew I was lucky to have Sammy to take care of things for me.

Coat on and bag in hand, I headed back into the café to go out through the front door. I smiled politely at my customers, saying hello here and there where it wasn't an interruption.

The two familiar-looking men were still sitting at their table. They still looked familiar, and to my frustration, I still couldn't place them. As I got closer though, I realized they were wearing matching gray shirts and black pants. And the shirts had patches on them. And then I had it. They were the museum security guards from the night of the heist.

Chapter Twelve

Like the worst investigator ever, I stopped dead in my tracks when I recognized who the security guards were. Right at their table too. They both looked up at me expectantly.

"Oh, um, I just realized, uh, um, that I know who you are." Brilliant, Fran.

They stared at me, presumably waiting for me to say something coherent and not totally weird.

"You're the security guards from the museum."

More staring.

"I saw you the other night. At the opening of the Cliffton exhibition."

Still staring.

"I just thought you looked familiar and—" I stopped myself. I was babbling like a fool. I needed to recover some of my dignity. "Let me start over. Hi, I'm Francesca Amaro, the owner of the café. I was just on my way out, but then I recognized you and wanted to stop and say hello. You're both from out of town, right?" When all else fails, fall back on the café-owner spiel.

"Yeah, we're from Boston," the younger looking of the two said, despite the fact that it was unnecessary to say where they were from as soon as the first word came out of his mouth. His Southie accent was so thick, you could probably hear it when he coughed.

"Well, welcome to Cape Bay!" I said, trying to sound cheerful and normal. "It's a little slow here this time of year, but hopefully you've been able to enjoy yourselves?" I inflected it as a question in an attempt to get them talking.

"Been working mostly." The younger one again. The older one had gone back to drinking his coffee. I was happy to note that his pie plate was scraped clean.

"Oh, that's too bad. Maybe you can come back sometime and really enjoy the town. It's not Boston, but it's a fun little place."

He nodded and picked up his coffee, perhaps taking a cue from his silent counterpart. I realized I was losing them, and I had to think of something fast if I wanted to try to get any information out of them. Honey could wait. These guys couldn't.

"It's a shame about that painting getting stolen, huh?"

Neither of them said anything, though the younger one flicked his eyes up at me briefly.

"Do you often provide security for museums? Is that something your company, uh"—I leaned to look at the patches on their shirts—"Kandinsky Security specializes in?"

"We do all kinds of security," the younger one said. "But, yeah, we do a lot of museums and stuff. I like it 'cause it's real educational, you know?"

I nodded hesitantly. I wasn't sure if he was being serious or just messing with me.

"Yeah, Butler here fancies himself a real Einstein," the older one said, finally looking up from his coffee. His accent was just as thick, if not thicker than the younger one's.

"Hey, you're one to talk! When we worked that history museum, I could never find you. You were always off looking at the exhibits."

"Oh, 'cause you've never followed some school kids around on a field trip so you could listen in on what the tour guide was sayin'."

"So you've guarded a lot of museums," I said quickly before they could bicker anymore.

"Yeah, we have," the younger one, Butler, said.

"Have you been working security long?"

"I got ten years, he's got twenty."

"Were you guys working when the painting was stolen?"

"Yeah, we were working," the older one said, suddenly hostile. "We were doin' our jobs. Not like it's any of your business."

"Oh, I didn't mean to say that you weren't doing your job! I just didn't know if it was you or someone else or if there were only guards when the gallery was actually open..."

I was really losing them now and didn't really know how to get them back.

"You think you can leave art like that unguarded? We got that place guarded twenty-four, seven. You don't know much about security, do you, lady?"

I hoped this was my opportunity. "No, I don't. That's why I'm hoping you can help me understand. What did you think of the security systems at the museum? Were they what you would expect for an exhibit of that caliber?"

The older one leaned towards me. "You got a lot of questions, don't you, lady? You're real curious, ain't you?"

I took a half step back, laughing nervously. "I've heard that once or twice."

"Yeah, maybe you should start to listen."

Now I took a whole step back. It was time to go. "You know, I think I will. It was good to meet both of you. If you'd like a refill of your coffees or a second slice of pie, it'll be on the house. Just let Sammy know you'd like some more." I stepped back again, smiled at each of them, and walked over to the counter to let Sammy know what I'd promised the guards.

Apparently, I'd been so involved in my conversation, I hadn't noticed the line forming behind me. We had a full-on rush. Honey B's would have to wait.

I hurried into the back room, dropped my coat and bag, threw my apron over my head, and headed back out to help Sammy.

I don't know if word had gotten around town about the pies or if everyone was just in the mood for coffee, but we were completely slammed for two solid hours.

We took orders from another six people for another eleven pies. Fortunately for my sanity, most of those were for Thanksgiving. Rhonda brought by the ice cream and ended up staying to help out. I was incredibly grateful for that because it gave me a chance to focus on the drinks which were my specialty.

The ice cream was a huge hit, and because of that or not, we were completely out of individual slices long before people stopped asking for them. By the time the rush was done, there was no way I could make it out to Honey B's, talk to Honey, come back, make the pies, and make it home before midnight. Instead, I let Rhonda take care of things in the front of the café while I worked on prepping, baking, and packaging pies.

Rhonda left after the café closed, and Matt came to keep me company. When I was finally done, he walked me home, and I collapsed onto the couch. Matt rubbed my aching feet while Latte lay on my chest and made up for all the love he'd missed out on in the hours I'd been gone.

I fell asleep and dreamt of pie, security guards, and egotistical aspiring novelists. I'd wanted to go by Honey B's on my way in to the café in the morning, but by the time I dragged myself out of bed, it was so late, I had to go straight in.

Rhonda was working again—Christmas was coming, and she wanted the extra money to subsidize her gift budget—and I worked alongside her and Sammy to get us through the lunch rush. By the time things calmed down and the café was all cleaned up and fully restocked, I knew I had pies to make, but I just wanted to take a break for a few minutes.

I sat down at the desk in the back room and poked around on the computer for a few minutes, checking my email, and then the news to see if there were any developments in the case that I hadn't heard about yet. There weren't, so I checked the status of the café's last supply order and put the next one through. I looked around the desk for the mail, but it wasn't where Sammy usually put it. I checked the time. It was well past when the mail usually came.

"Hey, Sammy?" I called, leaning back in my chair to try to project my voice out into the café.

"Yeah?"

"Has the mail come yet?"

"Oh, yeah, sorry, I put it on the shelf!"

I grabbed the mail off the shelf and sat back down to go through it. I sorted the envelopes into piles, the bills in one and everything else in another. One envelope was blank—no address, no return address, no stamp, no postmark. I flipped the envelope over. Nothing there either. But it was sealed, and there was something inside.

"Hey, Sammy?"

"Yeah?"

"What's this blank envelope?"

"I don't know. We were busy when it came in, so it sat on the counter for a while. Maybe somebody dropped something off?"

I slid the letter opener under the flap and cut the envelope open. I pulled out the single torn sheet of paper inside and felt my blood go cold as I read the words written on it.

"What is it?" Sammy asked from the doorway.

I stared at the paper, wondering if it meant what I thought it meant.

"Fran?" Sammy crossed the room to stand right behind me. "Fran, what is it? Is something wrong? Are you okay?"

"Um." I tried to put together words, but the single syllable was all I could get out. I tried to swallow, but my mouth had gone dry. "Um," I said again.

"Fran?"

"I think it's a threat." I held the paper up so she could see the single sentence printed on it in block letters:

Curiosity killed the cat.

Chapter Thirteen

"Oh, my God," Sammy whispered. "Do you think–do you think it's really a threat?"

"What else could it be?" I asked.

"A mistake?"

"A joke?"

"A bad one."

"Hey, what are you two–" Rhonda cut herself off in the middle of her sentence as she came into the room and saw us there. "Is everything okay?"

"Do you know anything about this?" I held the piece of paper out to her.

She crossed the room, holding out her hand to take it from me. As soon as she got close enough to read the words, she dropped her arm to her side. "What is that?"

"We don't know," Sammy said. "It came in the mail."

"It was *with* the mail," I clarified. "The envelope was blank. No name, no address, no postmark."

"Then where did it come from?" Rhonda asked. "It didn't just appear in the stack of mail. When did the mail even come?"

"It was at the beginning of that rush we had. The mail sat out on the counter by the register until I had a chance to grab it and bring it back." Sammy sounded nearly distraught.

"Anybody who came into the café would have been able to slip the envelope in there, and we were so busy we never would have noticed." Rhonda, for her part, sounded more thoughtful about it than anything. Not quite like she found it surprising, more like it was really interesting.

"Did you guys see anything unusual? Anyone who looked suspicious?" I asked.

Sammy shook her head rapidly, looking almost like she was fighting back tears.

"It was crazy in here, Fran," Rhonda said. "Sammy and I were running around like madwomen trying to take orders and get them filled and get the tables cleared off so people had a place to sit. George Clooney could have come in, and I don't think we would have noticed. You saw what it was like when you got here—it was probably twice as busy earlier this morning."

I couldn't blame them. I knew those days—the ones where you smiled in the direction of the customers, but were really looking at the empty napkin dispenser on the table behind them and the crumb-covered table next to that. On a normal day, I could tell you what somebody ordered three hours ago and what kind of latte art I used on it, kind of like the day before when Sammy had been able to immediately rattle off Brent Griffin's insanely complicated coffee order. When there was one of those crazy rushes though, I could take and fill an order and forget what it was by the time I delivered it to the table.

"I understand," I said. I took a deep breath. "And you know what? Maybe it's nothing. It's just a saying. People say it all the time. My mom must have said it ten times a day at Christmastime when I was a kid, and she certainly wasn't threatening me."

"Were you a snooper?" Rhonda asked.

"I wouldn't say that. I would say I was... observant."

"Let me guess, you opened up your mom's closet and *observed* what was on the top shelf hidden behind her sweaters."

I grinned. "Maybe."

"I guess old habits die hard, huh? You snooped then, you investigate now?"

Now I laughed. "I never thought about it, but, yeah, I guess that's true."

We heard the bell over the café's front door jingle. Rhonda peeked out to see if it was someone coming or going.

"Incoming," she said. "I'll go take care of them." She paused at the door. "You know, my boys have done treasure hunts around town with their sports teams. They go around and get weird clues and have to figure out where to go next. It could be something like that, and whoever dropped it off didn't think to tell us. Or they wanted to, and we were so busy they didn't get the chance."

"You know, you're probably right," I said. "It was probably something like that. Or somebody put it down and just forgot to take it with them."

"Exactly. Don't get yourself all wound up until you know there's something to be wound up about," Rhonda said and disappeared into the café.

"Do you really think it's nothing to worry about?" Sammy asked quietly.

I looked at the sheet of paper in my hand. "I—I don't know. But I don't want to make a big deal out of it and go running to Mike for it to turn out to be nothing. He already doesn't like me getting involved in his cases. If I started going to him with imaginary death threats I thought I was getting because of those cases, he'd be even more annoyed with me than he already is."

"Mike's not annoyed. He's just protective."

"Of his case, maybe."

"Of you! Remember how upset he got when you got that concussion?"

"I think he was more upset about getting blood all over his suit than he was about anything else."

"Oh, that's not true and you know it!"

I shrugged and tried to keep my half smile from becoming a whole one. "Okay, so maybe he's protective of me *and* his cases."

Sammy thought for a second. "Okay, I'll give you that," she said and laughed.

I knew she was right. Mike and I had known each other since we were little kids. He definitely wanted me to stay out of police business—he had been quite clear about that on more than one occasion—but I had also seen how scared he was several weeks earlier in the seconds between when I'd taken a brick to the head and when I passed out. For either reason, he wouldn't exactly be thrilled about me getting threats. And there would be a lecture for sure, whether it really was a threat or I just thought it was.

The more I thought about it, the more I figured that I was making something out of nothing. The envelope wasn't even addressed to me, for Pete's sake! Any of us could have picked it up and read it, although it was admittedly unlikely that it would be anyone other than Sammy or me. But still, I was the only one nosey enough to think that it had anything to do with me. If Sammy had opened it, she probably would have just thought it was some weird marketing campaign, which was actually a very logical explanation for what it was. If I asked the businesses around me, they probably got the same thing.

I slapped the paper and envelope down on the table. "You know what? I'm being ridiculous. There is absolutely no reason for me to think this is a threat, or that it's even directed at me." My voice came out with more confidence than I felt, but fake it 'til you make it wasn't a cliché for nothing.

Sammy smiled hopefully. "You really think so?"

Actually, I wasn't sure, but I was going to keep telling myself that I was. And besides, poor Sammy was a worrier. If she thought I was actually being threatened, she probably wouldn't be able to sleep at night for thinking about it. "I really think so."

She smiled a full-on Sammy smile. "Well, good. Because I'd hate to see anything happen to you. I'm finally getting you all trained up on how to run this place." She rubbed my shoulder affectionately.

"I'm sure you thought that before I forgot all about the fall menu too."

She giggled. "Yeah, I kind of did."

Rhonda poked her head in. "Hey, guys, could I get some help out here? A big group just came in."

"Sure thing!" Sammy chirped.

"I'll be right there," I said.

While Sammy went to help Rhonda with the customers, I arranged the stacks of mail neatly on the desk and set them to the side to deal with later. Left on the desk was the blank envelope and the sheet of paper with its cryptic message. I stared at them for a second then picked them up. My hand hovered over the trash can, ready to drop them in. But instead of letting them go, I put the paper back in the envelope, opened the desk drawer, and slipped the envelope in there. Just in case it really was a threat, it was better to hang on to it than to throw it away.

Confident that it was tucked safely away, I went out into the café to help Rhonda and Sammy. A flurry of customers, lattes, and pies later, I was locking up the café for the night. I'd called Honey Ballard during a lull a few hours before, and she'd told me—quite enthusiastically, in fact—that I was more than welcome to come over to Honey B's after I closed up the café for the night.

There was a chill in the November air, so I shoved my hands deep in my pockets to keep them warm as I made my way out to the edge of town to see Honey. It was just far enough that I briefly considered walking home to get my car and then driving out to her bed and breakfast, but I felt like I'd only been at the café or home (my house or Matt's—they were basically the same thing) in the past couple of days. A long walk through town would be nice. It would help me clear my head, and I could think about the case—or the Thanksgiving dinner I was supposed to host that I hadn't planned for at all yet.

Even though it wasn't that late, the streets were quiet. With it getting dark so early this time of year, it always seemed like it was later than it really was.

After about fifteen minutes of walking, I climbed the front steps of the big yellow Victorian that housed Honey B's B&B. She'd told me on the phone to just come in.

"Honey?" I called from the entrance-way. I knew it was a bed and breakfast—a business, just like mine—but it was also her home, and I didn't feel like it would be right to go in any further without being sure that she knew I was there.

"C'mon back, Fran!" Honey called from somewhere in the depths of the house.

To my right was a hallway lined with doors that I suspected were guest rooms. In front of me was a staircase. To my left was the parlor. Through a set of double French doors, I could see the dining room beyond it. It seemed most likely that Honey was back there somewhere.

I headed for the parlor, which was decorated with an abundance of flowers and bees. The pictures on the walls, the knickknacks on the mantel above the fireplace and scattered around the room— all flowers and bees. Even the abundant floral arrangements had bees tucked into them. Fake, of course. Little ceramic or resin bees, mounted on sticks and shoved down into the flower arrangements.

When I got close enough, I realized that the upholstery on the couch was a tiny honeycomb pattern. The curtains too. I glanced down at the rug covering the hardwood floor. It was probably the only hexagonal rug I'd ever seen, and it, too, was decorated with a honeycomb pattern. I was impressed with Honey's dedication to the theme.

I walked into the dining room. It was less obviously bee inspired, being more dedicated to dining than clutter, but sure enough, the pictures on the wall were of bees, either with their hives or with flowers. I was pretty sure one was a bee family portrait.

"Honey?" I called again.

"Right here!" The voice sounded like it was right on the other side of the swinging kitchen door.

I pushed it open just far enough to stick my head in. "Honey?"

"There you are!" Honey said exuberantly. "I would have come out to get you, but I'm a little messy. Have a seat!" She lifted her hands a few inches up out of the bowl they were in, and sure enough, they were covered with what looked like a very wet, sticky dough.

Honey, I guessed, was around my age, maybe a little younger, and exactly what you'd expect of someone named "Honey." She had warm-toned blond hair–honey-colored, you might say–and was sweet as, well, honey. I'd never seen her not busy (as a bee), zipping around town, darting in and out of shops to get the things she needed to take back to her hive—I mean, bed and breakfast—humming to herself all the while. When she wasn't humming, she liked to talk—a lot—about almost anything.

"What are you making?" I asked, pulling a stool up to the large kitchen island. The cabinets, I noticed were black, and the countertops were a warm-toned, almost yellowish granite. Dedication to the theme.

"Honey buns!"

I should have known. "For breakfast tomorrow?"

"Yup! Guests love 'em. I make them fresh every night."

Honey's accent was vaguely Southern, but no one knew where she was actually from—just that she hadn't grown up in Cape Bay. Unless maybe she moved to town when she was in high school, like some people swore. Those people couldn't remember whether her parents had been with her or, if not, who she'd lived with. Mostly, people agreed that she had moved to town in the past five or ten years. Other than that, she was a mystery. A pleasant, sociable mystery, but a mystery all the same. She was not, however, my mystery, so I wasn't worried about any of that today.

"Do you have many guests right now?" I asked, hoping it sounded totally smooth and off the cuff and not at all like getting information on one of her guests was the sole reason I was there. Of course, I didn't frequently make social calls on Honey— hadn't ever, to be honest—so the fact that I'd called and asked if I could come over for a chat was a pretty good tip-off that I was looking for information.

"Just one at the moment. Brent Griffin. Have you met him? He's Louis Cliffton's assistant. Cliffton, the artist with the show down at the museum." Honey was a font of detailed information. I could only hope that if I ever got myself involved in another investigation, Honey would have some information that pertained to it.

"I have met Brent, actually."

"Oh, so you know he's writing a novel, I guess." Honey laughed. "Yup, he sits down here at the writing desk in the parlor, tap-tap-tapping away on his laptop all the time. I'm surprised he's not there now. He's usually back by this time of night. I guess he must have stopped somewhere to get some supper. I don't serve supper, of course. It's a bed and breakfast, not a supper, bed, and breakfast." She laughed again.

"I heard Louis Cliffton was staying here also."

"Oh, yup, he is. But he's back in Boston right now. I can't say I'm surprised after that painting of his momma was stolen. Did you see that one? You were at the party Friday night, weren't you? Not really my kind of art, but I can see how some people would like it. Anyway, he booked his room for three weeks, but said he'd probably be coming and going, so I wasn't surprised he left. I expect he'll be back in the next day or two. No problem. He paid for the full three weeks up front. I certainly don't have a problem getting paid to keep a room for someone I don't have to cook for and clean up after!"

"How did Cliffton seem when he left? Was he upset about the painting being stolen?"

"Well, he seemed a little put out, but he's one of those real WASP-y stiff-upper-lip types, you know? Hard to get a good read on him."

"Did he take his things with him?"

"Just a little duffel bag, but that's about all he came in with too. He left a few little things up in his room though—a shirt and a pair of pants, a toothbrush and some toothpaste, some of those fancy artist pencils, and some paper on the desk. You know, Brent has a desk in his room too. I don't know why he doesn't work on his novel up there. Seems like it would be quieter. I'm always making a racket down here."

Because no one would know he was writing a novel if he worked on it in his room. I thought it, but I didn't say it. I didn't know Honey well enough to be sure she wouldn't repeat it, and it wasn't a very kind thing to say anyway.

"Does anything seem unusual or out of place in Cliffton's room?" I wanted to ask her if she could let me in to have a look around, but that felt intrusive. She had obviously already been in there to know what he'd left, so asking her about it would be the next best thing.

She stopped kneading her dough and raised an eyebrow at me. "You mean like a jewel-encrusted painting that's not supposed to be there?"

I was caught. Honey was going to shut down and not say another word to me about her guests.

Instead, she broke into a grin. "I know what you're about, Fran Amaro. You're like me—you're curious."

My heart slammed in my chest. There was that word again—*curious*. But it was just a word. People used it all the time.

"You know, they have that saying—curiosity killed the cat—"

My eyes darted around the room, looking for something I could use to defend myself if she came at me. But as my gaze flitted across her face, she looked every bit as friendly as she had when I first came in.

"But people always leave out the second part."

"Satisfaction brought it back," I said automatically.

"That's right!" Honey practically glowed with happiness. "That's you and me—we're curious, but the satisfaction of finding out what we want to know is what makes it all worth it!" She laughed happily and then leaned towards me conspiratorially. "So, I thought the exact same thing as you when Mr. Cliffton scurried out of here the morning after that painting was stolen. The bag he was carrying was too small to fit it in, so I went and gave his room a real thorough cleaning, just to make sure it was nice and fresh when he came back." She paused for a second. "You know, I would have done that anyway—a man shouldn't have to come back to slept-on sheets and dusty corners." Her eyes lit up again. "But this was a mystery, so it was exciting!"

"I guess you didn't find it?" I doubted it would happen, but part of me hoped that Honey would declare that of course she'd found it and whip it out from under the counter.

"Nope," she said, looking disappointed even as she said it.

"What about Brent's room?" I asked cautiously.

She sighed. "Oh, I looked there too. I looked all over this place. Not a million-dollar painting in sight."

We chatted for a few more minutes before I left with Honey's offer of fresh honey from the bees she kept. Because of course she did.

I headed back across town, wishing now that I hadn't decided against driving earlier. It had gotten later and chillier, and after a long, busy day, I was more than ready to curl up on the couch with a glass of wine and preferably a dog and a boyfriend. But I had a good mile-and-a-half walk ahead of me, and there was no use regretting my decision now. I could call Matt and ask him to come pick me up, but that would just make me feel silly. So I hunkered down and walked.

Cape Bay was quiet this time of year. Even though I'd grown up there, it still struck me as odd after spending so many years in New York. Some days, it felt nothing but peaceful. Other days, it felt almost sinister. When I thought about it, I suspected that it was because quiet streets in the city were a red flag more than anything. You wanted to be somewhere busy and populated, where all the witnesses would serve as a deterrent for would-be muggers.

Tonight, for some reason, the quiet streets of Cape Bay felt sinister. I chalked it up to the maybe-threat I'd received. But still, I walked a little quicker than usual.

I had just passed the Surfside Inn when I heard footsteps. I glanced behind me. No one. But the footsteps were gone too, so I told myself that whoever it was had gone into the motel.

I started walking again. After a few hundred feet, I heard the footsteps again.

This time, I kept walking for a few seconds to see what the footsteps would do. They sounded faster than mine, and they sounded like they were getting closer. I whirled around. Nothing.

I was almost to Main Street when I heard them again. I picked up my pace to get to the better lighting. The footsteps got closer. I spun around and then regretted where I'd chosen to stop. The orange-tinged lights of Main Street were bright, but half a block behind me was still shrouded in near-darkness. Unless whoever it was happened to be standing under a streetlight, I wouldn't be able to see them.

Still facing back towards where I'd come from and staring like I wasn't borderline night blind, I pulled my phone out of my pocket. I normally avoided talking on the phone while walking alone at night so that I wouldn't be distracted, but in this case, I was already pretty sure someone was following me, and my goal now was to make sure they knew I knew.

And to have someone on the other end to hear me scream.

Chapter Fourteen

Matt answered on the first ring. "Hey, gorgeous, what's up? You going to be home soon?"

"Hi, Matt," I said loudly. "I just wanted to let you know that I'm on Main Street, and I'll be home in just a few minutes." I stared into the dark.

"Um, is everything okay?"

"Yes, everything's just fine. I just wanted to let you know that I'm walking down Main Street, so I'll be home in a few minutes."

"Franny?"

I finally turned around and started walking towards home, my nonphone ear listening carefully for noises behind me. I spoke quietly into the phone. I wanted whoever was behind me to hear confident me, not nervous me. "I thought I heard someone walking behind me, and I wanted to make sure they knew that someone knew where I was and was expecting me."

"Is someone following you?" He sounded alarmed.

"Yes, no, well, I don't know. I keep thinking I hear footsteps, but when I turn around, there's no one there." My voice was still low.

"Do you hear footsteps now?"

"Um..." I tried to listen for them, but between the phone, my own footsteps, and my heavy breathing from my quick pace, I couldn't be sure. I didn't want to turn around to look either. "I don't think so. I'm not sure."

"Latte and I are coming to meet you. Don't move. No, do move. Keep walking. Stay on the sidewalk. No shortcuts, okay? Unless you feel like you'd be safer inside Antonia's? Are any of the other shops open?"

During tourist season, they all would have been, but tourist season was long over. "No, none of them are open. And I'd rather keep walking." I felt like if I stayed on the street, there was at least a chance of a car driving by. Locked inside Antonia's, I'd feel like a sitting duck, just waiting for whoever might be behind me to catch up or for someone to come save me. I preferred not to act like a damsel in distress.

"Then keep moving. Latte and I will meet up with you in a minute."

"You're going to stay on the phone with me, right?"

"Of course!"

We didn't talk much over the few minutes it took Matt to get to me, just an occasional update on where we were. Mostly, I listened. A couple of times, I thought I heard footsteps, but they stopped as quickly as they started. I told myself I was imagining things or turning echoes of my own footsteps into someone else's.

"Okay, I see you," Matt said through the phone.

I breathed a sigh of relief and punched the button to disconnect the call.

When Matt was close enough that we could clearly see each other, he dropped Latte's leash so he could run towards me. Which he did, except he kept running a couple of feet past me. He stopped there with his head hunched down and his ears flat back against his head. A low growl came from his throat as he stared off somewhere down the street.

"What's he doing?" Matt asked, coming up next to me.

"He's... growling at something." Latte wasn't a growler. He wasn't very vocal at all, except when I was in danger.

Matt turned his gaze down the street.

"Do you see anything?" I asked after a few seconds.

"No, do you?"

I shook my head then realized that he wasn't looking at me and said no out loud.

"Let's go," Matt said. He bent down and picked up Latte's leash. Latte, whose hackles were still up, only reluctantly turned around when I started walking away. Apparently, staying with me was more important than keeping whatever was behind us at bay.

I slipped my hand into Matt's as we walked back towards home. He and Latte both turned around periodically to check behind us. I avoided it. I trusted the two of them to keep me safe.

Within minutes we were walking up to my house.

"I'm coming in with you," Matt announced.

I had no problem with that. I was both still a little spooked and more than happy to spend some time with Matt.

Inside, Matt hovered at the window for a few minutes.

"What are you doing?" I asked, my voice not rising above a whisper.

"Watching."

"Do you see anything?" I slipped my arms around his waist and rested my head against his back. He rubbed my hands with his.

"No, but that doesn't mean there's nothing out there."

"It could have just been my imagination. You never heard anything behind us, did you?"

"Latte thought something was back there."

Latte's ears perked up beside us at the sound of his name. I reached down and scratched his head.

"It could have been a squirrel," I said.

"Does Latte growl at squirrels?"

"Maybe it was a raccoon then." I didn't really believe it, but I didn't want to believe that someone had been following me either. "It could have been someone else walking home."

Matt rubbed my hands again. "I guess you're right." He turned around and wrapped me in his arms. "I just can't stand the thought of anything happening to you." We stood like that for a while, holding each other, until Matt broke our reverie. "I guess I better go check the house." He flipped the living room light on. We'd been standing in darkness until then.

"You're going to check the house?"

"Yup, and you're going to follow me."

"Whoever it was—if it even was anyone—would still be outside, not inside," I told him.

"I'm not taking any chances," he said.

He made his way around the house, making sure I was close behind him, and turned on every light, looked inside every closet, and checked every window and door lock. When the place was finally lit up brighter than it probably ever had been—my grandparents and mother had always been firmly in the "leave a room, turn off the lights" camp—he was finally satisfied. "You want me to start a fire?"

I nodded. The house was on the chilly side, and I knew I wasn't going to be going to bed anytime soon, so there was no reason not to. Besides, it would be romantic. We could drink wine, curl up by the fire, relax, and just enjoy being a couple.

"Okay, but I can't stay late. I have to head up to Boston early tomorrow, remember?"

No, I hadn't remembered, but now I did. Matt had two solid days of meetings with a new client up in Boston. He wasn't even going to be coming back to Cape Bay the next night, even though it was only an hour and a half away. There was going to be a big client dinner that they expected to go late, and then of course, the meetings started back up early the next morning. His company was putting him up in a hotel for the night.

"You forgot, didn't you?"

I nodded.

"I guess that just means we have to make the most of the time we have." He slipped his arms around me, pulling me close, and kissed me.

A few hours, a couple glasses of wine, and a cozy fire later, I was in bed with Latte curled up next to me. I slept fitfully, rolling over what felt like every few minutes, trying, mostly unsuccessfully, to get comfortable. I was hot, then I was cold. The T-shirt I was sleeping in was getting all wrapped around me. Latte was taking up too much space. It felt like I had only just fallen asleep when my cell phone rang on my nightstand.

I fumbled for it. It was still dark out. Who on earth was calling me when it was still dark out? I looked at the display. Sammy. Suddenly worried, I answered it.

"Sammy? What's going on? Is everything okay?"

"Everything is fine. I'm sorry to wake you, but you need to come down to Antonia's."

"If everything is fine, why are you calling me at—what time is it anyway?"

"It's just after five."

Just after five. That meant Sammy had probably just gotten to the café to open it up for the day. "Sammy, what's going on? Everything can't be fine if you're calling me at five in the morning. Is it something with the café?"

"Fran, I just need you to come down here." Sammy's voice was troublingly measured. She was usually bubbly and exuberant, but every word sounded like it was coming out now very deliberately.

Then a horrifying thought struck me. "Sammy, are you safe?"

"Yes, I'm safe. I'm fine. I just need you here at the café as soon as possible." Whatever it was, she wasn't going to tell me over the phone.

"Okay, I'll be there as soon as I can. I just need to get dressed." I was already out of bed, pulling clothes out of my closet with one hand. I didn't care if it matched or looked good together–I just needed clothes that would go on my body and keep me relatively warm.

"Okay, good."

"I'll see you soon. Bye." I was just about to pull the phone away from my head when I heard Sammy's voice again.

"Oh, and Fran?"

"Yeah?"

"Don't be freaked out if you see police cars out here."

Chapter Fifteen

I drove instead of walking. I didn't think I had ever in my life driven to the café, but if Sammy was calling me at five o'clock in the morning, the couple of minutes' difference driving would make in how quickly I got to the café mattered.

I couldn't drive all the way to the café though. A police car was parked in the middle of the road a block away from it. Now I was even more concerned.

I pulled my car up to the curb in an approximation of parallel parking, jumped out, and ran down the street towards Antonia's. A police officer stopped me before I could reach the café.

"Whoa there, ma'am. Where're you going in such a hurry?" he asked.

"The café! I need to get to the café!"

"Café's closed, ma'am. You'll have to get your coffee fix somewhere else."

Closed? My café was closed? "No, you don't understand! I'm the owner! I need to get to the café!"

"Fran? Fran, is that you?" I heard Sammy's voice calling me from somewhere down the street.

"Sammy! I'm right here! Sammy!" I was jumping, trying to see her over the policeman's hulking shoulders. I bounced back and forth, trying to get past him, but he held his arms out, blocking my way. "Let me go!" I shouted at him.

"Let her through, Pollack!" Never in my life had I been so grateful to hear Mike's voice.

"Mike! What's going on?" I asked.

"I need to ask you a few questions, Fran."

"What? What are you talking about? What's going on with the café?"

"Just come over here for a minute." He took my arm and guided me in the wrong direction—across the street and away from the café.

"No, Mike, I need to get to the café. Sammy called me. I need to get to the café."

"I just need to ask you a few things first."

Then I realized what was going on. Something was wrong at the café, and Mike needed to hear my answers to his questions before I saw it. He either thought I would be too upset to talk after I saw it or thought I was involved. I let him lead me across the street.

"What time did you leave Antonia's last night, Fran?"

I swallowed hard. My nerves were making it hard to talk. "Um, after closing. Around seven."

"And were you the last one to leave?"

"Yes, of course."

"I have to ask the questions, Fran."

I nodded.

"Was anyone with you when you left?"

"No."

"You closed up by yourself?"

"Yes."

"When did the last customer leave?"

"About ten minutes before me. Just before seven. I'd already done most of the cleaning up, so I just had to do a couple things before I left."

"Did you go out the front or the back?"

"The front."

"Did you see anyone on the street when you left?"

"Not really, no."

Mike raised an eyebrow.

"I mean, no. I didn't see anyone else. I remember thinking that it seemed later than it really was because of how dark out it was."

He nodded. "And did you go straight home?"

"No. I went out to Honey Ballard's."

"I didn't know the two of you were friends."

I could either lie or tell the truth and get a lecture. But friend or no, Mike was the police, and he was the only thing standing between my café and me. "Um, we're not."

Mike clenched his jaw. "Then I guess you know that's where Brent Griffin and Louis Cliffton are staying."

"Yes," I said quietly.

Mike sighed and closed his eyes for a second. "I think it's time you see the café."

A wave of nervousness washed over me. I didn't like something about the way he said it.

He started walking back towards the café, waving at me to follow him. He stopped, just before the crime scene van, blocking my view of the café, and looked back over his shoulder at me. Then he stepped aside.

I gasped and clapped my hands over my mouth. An icy-cold wave of fear swept through me. My knees felt weak, and I wanted to throw up. I felt Mike's arm go around me with just enough pressure to hold me up. It wasn't what had happened that was shaking me. It was what it meant.

Curiosity killed the cat was emblazoned across the front windows of the café in red spray paint, accompanied by a cartoonish dead cat, complete with Xs over the eyes.

"Oh, my God," I whispered. If it wasn't for Mike's arm around me, I probably would have fallen to the pavement.

"I assume that wasn't there when you left last night."

"No."

"There doesn't appear to be any forced entry, but we need to go in and take a look around before we can let you and Sammy in. Do you have your keys?"

"Yeah, they're on my key ring." I reached into my empty pocket for them. "I must have left them in the ignition." I turned to go back down the block towards my car, but Mike stopped me.

"Pollack!" he called.

"Yes, sir?"

"Go get Franny's keys out of her car and bring them up here."

"Yes, sir!"

"Let's let you sit down," he said and guided me past the café over to where his minivan was parked next to a squad car.

"You brought the minivan?" I asked.

He shrugged. "It was behind my car in the driveway."

I really looked at him for the first time. His hair was a mess, and his eyes were puffy with sleep. He had on track pants, sneakers, and a Cape Bay Police sweatshirt. He must have rolled out of bed and come straight here.

"Fran!" Sammy jumped up from where she was sitting on the curb and ran over to hug me.

I held on to her and fought back tears.

"I'm so sorry to have woken you up, but I knew you'd want to know right away."

"It's fine, Sammy. You did the right thing."

"Sammy, I think Fran needs to sit down," Mike said.

Sammy led me over to the curb and sat down next to me. We sat in silence for a couple of minutes until I found my voice.

"I'm so sorry," I said quietly.

"For what?" she asked. "You didn't do it."

"No, but I'm the reason it happened."

"You're not responsible for anyone's actions but your own."

I looked over at her. She looked neat and pulled together and wide awake in contrast to my messy, haphazard self. "My actions are what led to this."

She put her arm around me. "It's not your fault, Fran."

I didn't deserve a friend like her.

We sat there on the curb for what seemed like an eternity while the police went over the café with a fine-toothed comb. I called Matt once I thought he'd be awake to let him know what was going on.

"Do you think this is related to whoever was following you last night?" he asked.

"I don't know. Maybe."

"Have you told the police about it?"

"Not yet. I haven't had much of a chance to talk to Mike."

"But you're going to, right?"

"Yes."

"Promise?"

"Promise." I took a deep, shaky breath. I also planned to tell Mike about the note I'd received the previous day, but I hadn't mentioned that to Matt, and I wasn't about to tell him now. Not with him about to leave town.

"Do you want me to come down there? For moral support?" he offered.

"No, your meetings are important. You need to go up to Boston."

"I can reschedule."

"No, you need to go. I'll be okay. It's not like anything was permanently damaged. I'm sure we'll be opening up soon."

"Are you sure?"

"I'm sure."

"Keep me updated?"

"Of course."

We said we loved each other and hung up.

I looked around the street. As the town had started waking up, more and more people had come out to see what was going on. I spotted Mary Ellen Chapman from the gift shop across the street standing near us. "I have an idea," I told Sammy.

I went to find Mike, and with his permission and Mary Ellen's assistance, Sammy and I started making coffee in Mary Ellen's coffee pot and handing it out to people. It wasn't the quality of the café's coffee, but people seemed to appreciate the gesture, especially the police officers who'd been out there in the cold for going on two hours. Mike seemed particularly grateful, draining both the cups I'd taken over to him in quick succession.

As he handed them back to me, he shook his head with a wry smile. "It's good, but it's not what I get from Antonia's. Promise me the first cup when you open up."

"On the house," I replied. Neither of us mentioned that police officers and fire fighters always got free coffee. "By the way, do you know when that will be?"

He ran his hand through his messy hair. "We're finishing up. You and Sammy will be allowed in soon. You have cameras, right?"

"Yup." I nodded.

"We'll need your help to look at those." He looked around at the people gathered around to watch the police work. "It'll be a little while before you can open back up though. Probably midmorning."

"Thanks. I appreciate you taking it seriously." Vandalism wasn't an unheard-of problem in Cape Bay. This was a little more extreme than most cases, but I was glad they weren't brushing it off.

Mike sighed and shoved his hands in his pockets. "Franny, I think you know that we think this is associated with the art theft."

I nodded.

"Whoever took the painting probably thinks you're on to them, and they're trying to scare you off."

I swallowed hard but nodded again.

"Before we let you open back up, I need to talk to you and get a detailed list of everyone you've talked to about this case and what you've discussed with them."

"Absolutely."

He looked at me like he wanted to say something else, but he clenched his lips. "I'll let you and Sammy know when you can go back in," he said finally.

"Thanks," I said, and went back to serving coffee. It was a comforting and familiar action. If I couldn't be inside the café, at least I could act like it.

The crowd on the street had begun thinning out when Mike came over to Sammy and me. "You two ready to get inside?" he asked.

We went happily. The sun had never quite come out, staying well-hidden behind a thick layer of clouds, and we were both more than ready to get inside somewhere with heat. Walking around and carrying hot cups of coffee had helped fend off the chill, but not enough.

I got the tapes from the security cameras for Mike, and then he sat us down in the café with our backs to the front window, I guessed so that we didn't have to look at the spray painting while we talked. I told him about everyone I'd talked to and what they said, and he took notes in the little notebook he carried with him everywhere. I gave him the list of people I suspected even a little: Brent, Cliffton, the guards, and Adam. I made sure he knew that I hadn't actually gotten the chance to talk to Adam yet. And that I didn't really think Cliffton did it but had checked into him all the same.

"Is that it? Is there anything else?" he asked when I'd finally finished.

Sammy and I exchanged a look.

"What is it?" I couldn't tell if he sounded frustrated or tired.

"Um, I got a note yesterday," I said, staring at my hands.

"A note?"

I nodded.

"What kind of note?"

"Well, at first I thought it was a threat, and then I thought I was being ridiculous, but then—" I gestured at the window behind me.

"Do you still have it?"

I nodded.

"Show me."

I stood up and led him to the back room and over to the desk. "It's in here," I said, opening the desk drawer.

"Stop," Mike said. "Don't touch it."

I froze.

"Do you have gloves? Any kind—latex, food service?"

I grabbed a pair from the shelves behind him and handed them over. He slipped them on and went over to the desk. "This it?" he asked, pulling out the envelope I'd stashed in there the day before.

I nodded.

Holding the envelope by its edges, he slid the note out. I watched his face. It was unreadable at first, then he closed his eyes and exhaled. When he opened them again, he looked at me.

"Why didn't you call me as soon as you got this?" he asked.

I debated which version of the truth made me sound least like a complete idiot. I decided on the most true option—the one that covered all the others. "I didn't want to believe it was really a threat."

He closed his eyes and took another deep breath.

"I mean, it wasn't addressed to me. And it didn't have any markings on it. And—"

"Franny." He sounded tired. So very, very tired.

"Yeah?"

"You're not one to cry wolf. If anything, you're too calm about things. If you think something might be a threat, it's suspicious enough that you need to report it."

"Okay." I felt like a child. But not in a bad way. In a "you should have trusted your parents" kind of way.

"I need to get this to the lab." He whipped an evidence bag out of his pocket and dropped the envelope and paper in.

"You keep evidence bags in your pocket but not gloves?" I knew I probably shouldn't have said it, not at that moment anyway, but it was so strange I couldn't stop myself.

He shrugged as he scribbled on the bag's label with a permanent marker he'd somehow procured. "Some days I have evidence bags, some days I have gloves. Some days I even have toy cars. Or glitter. It's a crapshoot." He finished filling out the label and looked at me. "Who knows about this?"

"Sammy, Rhonda, and me."

"That's it? You didn't tell Matt?"

"I didn't want him to worry."

"There is such a thing as being too independent, Fran."

"I know."

"All right, well, you're free to clean off the window. Leary's coming off duty, so I'm sure that if Sammy asks him to, he'll be happy to come over and take care of scraping it all off." Leary, of course, was Ryan's last name.

I smiled. "Strictly platonically, of course."

"Of course," Mike replied. Ryan and Sammy's nonrelationship relationship was just as obvious to Mike as it was to everyone else, and I knew he teased Ryan about it just as much as we teased Sammy. Probably more, actually, knowing him.

"If you don't mind fixing me one for the road, I'll be on my way, and you two can work on opening this place up." He started towards me and the door, but I didn't move. I stared at my shoes.

"Um, there is one other thing."

"What is it?" he asked wearily.

"Last night on my way home from Honey B's, I think someone might have been following me."

"And why do you think that?" His voice was tight and measured.

"I heard footsteps. I looked behind me, but no one was there."

"It was just once? You heard footsteps, and then they stopped?"

"It was a couple of times."

He sighed. "Where were you?"

"It started when I was right past the Surfside Inn, and I was on Main Street the last time I heard it. That's when I called Matt, and he and Latte came to walk me the rest of the way home."

"You heard footsteps behind you all the way from the Surfside to Main Street, and you didn't call anyone—not Matt, not the police—until you were on Main Street?"

"I only heard them on and off."

"On and off," he repeated then swore under his breath. "Franny, look," he said, taking a step closer to me. "I know I tell you this all the time, and you never listen, but this is different. Franny, someone doesn't like you getting involved with this case. I don't know who it is or why, but if they've gone from anonymous notes to following you to vandalizing your place of work in less than twenty-four hours, we're dealing with someone who is not afraid to escalate. You have to back off. Your life could be in danger if you don't."

I swallowed hard and nodded. There were tears in my eyes because I knew he was right.

"I'm not trying to scare you, but fifteen years of police work have taught me that this kind of behavior is serious. I know it was a beautiful painting, and I know you get going and you don't want to stop until you solve the case, but this is a matter for people with guns and badges, not coffee and pie, okay?"

I nodded.

"And if anything else remotely suspicious happens, you call me immediately, okay? I don't care what time of night it is or how insignificant you want to convince yourself that it is."

I nodded again.

"Lock your doors, and don't walk alone at night."

Another nod.

"Now make me a cup of coffee so I can get out of here and find this guy."

Chapter Sixteen

Sammy tried to send me home so I could go back to sleep, but I knew that would be impossible, so I stayed to help her get the café straightened back up and opened for business.

I'd wanted to wait until the threatening graffiti was cleared off the window to open, but customers started arriving as soon as the police cars were gone, so in the end, we went ahead and opened up. It's not like the whole town wasn't going to see or hear about the spray-painted window anyway. Besides, as predicted, Ryan was coming over with a razor blade to start scraping as soon as he went home and got changed.

Unsurprisingly, almost every customer wanted to talk about the vandalism. For the most part, Sammy and I just shrugged and said that the police were investigating. We talked a little more to the people we knew a little better but still avoided getting into details. Partly because Mike had warned us not to talk about it, and partly because we just didn't want to.

All the excitement and Cape Bay's general nosiness made us busier than usual which, to be honest, I was grateful for. I didn't want a lot of downtime. I didn't want to think about the events of the past twenty-four hours.

"Hey, gorgeous."

I looked up sharply at the next customer in line. "Matty!" I couldn't help myself; I ran around the counter and threw myself into his arms. He was exactly the person I needed at the moment. "What are you doing here?" I asked when I had soaked up enough of his love that I felt like I could get through the next few minutes without burying my face in his chest again. "You're supposed to be in Boston!"

He shrugged and grinned at me, his warm brown eyes making me feel just as safe and loved as his arms had. "I told my boss I had an emergency at home and I wouldn't be able to make it. Well, until after lunch. I really do have to be there for that meeting. Unless you need me, of course. I'm not that important."

"Yes, you are."

"To them, I mean."

I smiled and snuggled back into him. I was fairly certain he really was that important to them too, but I was happy that I came first in his book.

"I'll help the next person in line!" I heard Sammy say and realized we were standing right in the middle of the café. I grabbed Matt's hand and dragged him into the back, where he promptly kissed me.

"So are you okay?" he asked me after several blissful seconds that made me forget why he was asking.

"Yeah. A little shaken up, but yeah."

"Good." He caressed my back. "Does Mike have any idea who did it?"

"He thinks it was whoever stole the painting. That they don't like me being involved, and they're trying to scare me off."

"Did you tell him about the person following you last night?"

I nodded my head against his chest.

"What did he say?"

"That the next time something remotely suspicious happens, I need to call him immediately."

"And you're going to listen to him?"

I nodded again.

"Franny," Matt said as he very gently pushed me away from him so he could look me in the eye. "You know I don't want to be one of those guys who tells you what to do and expects you to listen to me because I'm your boyfriend, but—"

"You don't have to say it. I'm done."

"You are?"

"Yes. I'm out of it. I don't want anything else to do with this case. Or any case, for that matter. Mike said this is a job for guns and badges, and he's right."

"Good," he said and pulled me into him again. "I don't know what I'd do if something happened to you."

He held me like that until Sammy popped her head into the back.

"Hey, Fran? Sorry to interrupt, but Ryan's here. Is it okay for him to get started on the window?"

"Sure, tell him to go ahead."

"Does he need help?" Matt asked.

"I don't think he'd turn it down," Sammy said. "It's going to be a pretty big job."

"Tell him I'll be right out."

"Great! I will." Sammy ducked back into the café, leaving Matt and me alone again.

"Ryan's here to clean the window off, huh? I guess that's just a part of his job as a law enforcement officer?"

I giggled. "Yup. And I'm sure Sammy asking him to help had absolutely nothing to do with it."

"I'm sure." He grinned at me. "Think I could get a cup of coffee before I head out there? I was going to order one, but then this cute girl kind of tackled me, and I lost my place in line."

"Oh, I think we could manage that."

"How much is coffee running now?" he asked, sliding his arms back around me.

"Roughly one kiss," I said, and his mouth covered mine.

I got him his coffee and sent him outside armed with a box cutter, a spray bottle, and a towel to use to clean the paint off the window. Ryan started on the morbid cat while Matt worked on the word "killed." Apparently, they'd decided to focus on the most objectionable portions first.

I'd hardly gotten back to work when Rhonda came in the door. She completely skipped the line and walked right around the counter to Sammy and me. "Are you two okay?"

"Yes, we're fine. Neither of us was here when it happened," I said for what felt like the hundredth time that day. Most of our more polite customers—the ones who were concerned but didn't want to come across like they were prying for information—took the route of asking us how we were.

"I know that, but that doesn't mean you're okay," Rhonda said.

Sammy and I glanced at each other, and I dragged Rhonda into the back. "We're fine. The police are handling it," I said.

"You told them about the note?" she asked.

I wondered what vibe I gave off that had everybody thinking they had to confirm that I'd told the police everything. "Yes, I told them about the note."

"And what did they say?"

"Exactly?"

"You can paraphrase."

"That I'm too independent for my own good, and I need to report things like that."

"I take it you talked to Mike."

"That obvious, huh?"

Rhonda laughed. "He's not a subtle man."

"No, he is not," I agreed.

"So are you really okay?" she asked after a few seconds. "It was more than just vandalism."

"Yeah, I think so. I don't know if I'll be able to sleep tonight, but I didn't fall asleep until after two, and Sammy called me at five, so sheer exhaustion might just win out over fear."

"Matt's going to stay with you, right?"

I shook my head. "No, he's going out of town."

"Tonight? After his girlfriend's life just got threatened? Do I need to go have a chat with him?"

"No, it's fine, Rhonda. He's actually already supposed to be there, but he told his boss there was an emergency so he could make sure I was okay."

"Where's he going?"

"Boston."

"So you're going up with him then?"

"No! I'm not leaving the café. I'm not running away like I'm scared. I'll let the case go, but I'm not letting whoever this person is scare me away from the business my grandparents built."

Rhonda studied me for a few seconds then nodded and smiled. "I like it when you show a little backbone. It suits you."

"Thanks, I guess."

"Do you want to stay at my house tonight so you don't have to be alone?"

"Thank you for the offer, but I'll be fine. I have Latte to protect me."

"That vicious dog?" Rhonda laughed.

"Hey, he can bark up a storm when he wants to."

She laughed again. "I'm sure he can. But you're more than welcome to stay if you change your mind."

"I'll keep that in mind," I assured her, although I had no intention of taking her up on it. I wasn't going to run scared to

Boston, and I wasn't going to run scared to Rhonda's house.

"Who's closing with you tonight?"

"No one. You know I usually close alone." I wasn't sure what she was getting at, and I wasn't sure yet whether I would like it.

"Well, not tonight, you're not. Is Becky working this afternoon?"

"Yes, but I'm not asking her to stay until close."

"I wouldn't want you to. Not with this mess going on." She waved her hand out towards the café. "I'll come in as soon as Dan gets home and close up with you. What time is it?" She glanced at her expensive-looking wristwatch. I wondered if she'd managed to buy it on what I paid her or if she'd convinced her husband, Dan, to buy it for her. "Geez, I have to go. I have to go to the dentist. I'll see you tonight." She turned to go, but I stopped her.

"I don't need you to come in to babysit me."

"I'm not babysitting you. I'm watching out for you. And don't try to argue with me because I'm not having it. I may not be able to make you stay at my house tonight, but this is a public place, and even if you won't let me work, I know you're not going to kick me out. I'll see you tonight. Oh, and I'm driving you home too." She walked out before I could say anything. "Bye, Sammy. Take care!" I heard her say as she breezed by Sammy.

"Everything okay?" Sammy asked as I walked up beside her.

"Rhonda's insisting on closing up with me tonight and driving me home."

"Good," Sammy replied. "You shouldn't be here on your own."

"What? You're turning on me too?"

"I'm not turning on you. I'm watching out for you."

"That's exactly what Rhonda said."

"And she's right. You know you wouldn't let any of us close up alone tonight, so why should we let you? If Rhonda wasn't going to be here with you, I'd come back in. It's not safe. Not right now."

I stared at her for a second. She wasn't usually so forceful. The words sounded strange coming out of her cherubic face.

"Fine," I sighed, giving in. I didn't really want to admit it to myself, let alone anyone else, but I was glad they didn't want to leave me alone. Whether I liked it or not, the threats had me spooked.

Chapter Seventeen

After lunch, things thankfully started to calm down a little. All the real looky-loos had come and gone shortly after we opened, and we were down to just a few scattered local regulars and Brent.

I didn't know when he'd snuck in, but there he was, in the corner, typing away at his laptop. He was dedicated, that was for sure. Maybe not to his boss, but at least it was to something.

Ryan and Matt had finished their laborious scraping of the paint off the window and were wiping it down with window cleaner and rags.

"It looks good," Sammy said, catching me watching them.

"They did a good job," I agreed.

"It doesn't seem like it should be that easy to clean up though, does it? For as awful as it was."

I shook my head. "I feel like I should feel better now that it's gone, but it's almost worse. Like there's no evidence of why I feel bad, so why aren't I over it yet?"

Sammy nodded. "I feel the same way."

I wondered how she did feel. I was obviously the one who'd been threatened, but she'd been the one who found it, standing alone on the street in the dark of early morning. She hadn't known whether the person who'd done it was gone or lurking just around the corner or inside the café. That had to be pretty terrifying too.

The guys outside stood back to admire their handiwork. They smiled at us through the window. We smiled back. They waved us out.

"How's it look?" Ryan asked proudly.

"Really good," I said. "I think it's cleaner than it was yesterday."

"Matt here's the man with the squeegee." Ryan thumped Matt on the back.

"My dad had me do the windows at his barbershop pretty much from the time I could stand up. I've had a lot of practice."

"You did good work," I said, slipping my arm around him. He kissed me on the top of the head. Ryan just stood there next to Sammy with his hands in his pockets like it was taking everything he had not to touch her. "I think they deserve coffee and pie, what do you think, Sammy?"

"Coffee and pie it is!" she replied.

Before we could get inside, I spotted the two security guards from the museum approaching us. Not sure if they were headed for the café, I stood by the door and waited as they approached.

They didn't come in, but they didn't ignore me either. Instead, the older one smirked at me. "Looks like you really don't know anything about security, huh, lady?" he said as he nodded at the newly clean window.

My stomach felt sick. I went into the café and headed straight for the back room.

"Fran? Are you okay?" Ryan asked as I blew past him and Matt.

I didn't answer.

"Franny, what's wrong?" Matt asked, following me into the back. "What happened? Did those guys say something to you?"

"I–I don't know. I mean, yes, one of them said something, but I don't know if it was something to worry about or if I'm making a big deal out of nothing."

"What did he say?"

I looked up at him. It sounded ridiculous, but if I couldn't sound ridiculous with Matt, who could I sound ridiculous with? "He looked at the window and said, 'I guess you really don't know anything about security.'"

Matt's face darkened, and his jaw started to clench.

"That's not what bothered me," I said quickly.

"Then what was it?" He still seemed like he wanted to go after the security guard.

"It's just that–" I hesitated. It sounded ridiculous. "The window was clean. I mean, maybe he saw it earlier, but maybe–" I stopped myself before I said it.

"We need to call Mike," Matt said, reaching in his pocket for his phone.

"No." I put my hand on his arm to stop him.

"Yes, we do. It may be nothing, but it may be something. He'd want to know. We need to call."

"No, *we* don't," I said. "I do. I know you want to take care of me, Matty, but whoever this is is trying to intimidate me. I'll give up the case, but I won't let myself be cowed into letting my boyfriend call the police for me. I need to do this for myself, if only to prove to Mike that I listened to him."

Matt looked at me, obviously thinking over what I'd said. I knew he wanted to be my protector, and truthfully, I wanted that too. But I was scared, and the best way I knew to stop being scared was to stand up for myself. Finally, he put his phone back in his pocket.

I got mine out and dialed Mike's number.

"Mike Stanton," he said by way of greeting.

"Mike, it's Fran."

"What's going on? Is everything okay?"

"Everything's fine, something just happened that I thought I should tell you about."

"Is it urgent? We're right in the middle of reviewing the footage from your cameras. I can swing by as soon as we're done."

"That's fine. Or you can just call me back. It's nothing I can't explain over the phone."

"I'll come by. I could use a fresh cup of coffee that doesn't taste like the sludge we have around here."

I wondered if Mike would be at Antonia's as much if the police department had decent coffee. And then I wondered what excuse Ryan would cook up for coming to see Sammy. It almost made it tempting to go over there and give them a coffee-making class. But that was neither here nor there. "Okay, I'll see you in a little bit. Bye."

Matt looked at me expectantly, having only heard my half of the conversation.

"He's looking at the video from the security cameras, and then he's going to be over to talk to me and get some coffee," I said.

"Are you okay with that?" he asked.

I nodded.

"Okay, then so am I." He took a deep breath. "Are you okay with me going to Boston? I can beg off if I need to. Or I can come back after the dinner tonight and then head back out early tomorrow."

"No, it's okay," I said, stroking his arm. "You go. I'll be fine here. The girls will be sure of that. Rhonda's already insisted on closing with me tonight, and she's trying to get me to sleep at her house."

"It would be a good idea."

"I'm a big girl. I'll be fine."

His big brown eyes looked down into my blue ones. "Just call me tonight so I know you're safe, okay?"

I nodded.

"And in the morning."

"Okay."

"And any time before, after, or in between that you feel like it."

My lips curved into a smile. "I will."

"Promise?"

"I promise."

I sank into him as he kissed me. I was going to miss him more than a little.

"Want me to drive your car back to the house?" he asked.

"Sure," I replied. "It'll make it easier for Rhonda to drive me home."

"I'll take Latte for a quick walk too."

"I love you."

"You can say that when I'm not offering to walk your dog."

"I love you then too."

Matt smiled and kissed me again. "Now how about that coffee and pie?"

I sat with Matt while he ate what I was pretty sure was his lunch, and then sent him off to Boston with another cup of coffee and a chocolate cupcake for the road. Matt's love for my chocolate cupcakes bordered on exceeding his love for me.

After I waved goodbye, I made my way around the café, checking on customers and straightening up tables. Brent Griffin was still at his table, and as much as I would have liked to avoid him, I knew it would be rude. And rude was the one thing I had been raised to never be towards customers.

"Hi, Brent, how are you?" I asked, coming up to his table.

He looked up at me languidly, as though reluctant to tear himself away from his novel. He smiled. "Francesca. I heard you had a bit of excitement here today. That must have been very upsetting for you."

I gave him my café-owner smile. "It was, but it's all cleaned up now, so we're ready to get things back to normal."

"That's very brave of you. I saw the window before it was cleaned. Do you think it was just some random graffiti, or was someone trying to send you a message?" He gave me a sniveling little smile that I wished was socially acceptable to smack off his face.

I did my best to smile back pleasantly. "You know, I don't know, but either way, it wasn't a very nice thing for someone to do." *And neither was asking that question*, I thought. And now, despite my better judgement, I was also going to do something that wasn't very nice. "How's Mr. Cliffton doing? It must be very upsetting for him that his painting hasn't been found yet."

"I wouldn't know. He went back to Boston on Saturday, and I've hardly heard from him since. Apparently, he expects me to be the liaison with the police who gets it all handled."

"Well, I'm sure he means it as a compliment. After all, he trusted you to spec out the security system too, didn't he?" I smiled sweetly. "Now, is there anything else I can get you?"

"No. Thank you."

I noticed that there was not a single dish on his table. Not a coffee cup, not a plate. Either Sammy had already been by to clear the dishes for him, or he hadn't ordered a thing. I suspected the latter. Normally, I don't mind it if people come in just to read or work without ordering anything when the café's not busy, but Brent doing it irked me. So I kept smiling. "Well, if you change your mind, just let us know." And I cheerfully walked away.

"Do you mind if I take a quick break?" Sammy asked as I walked around to where she was standing behind the counter.

"Go right ahead," I told her.

She slipped her apron off over her head and headed out the front door and across the street. Ryan wasn't standing far enough to the side that I couldn't see him. The two of them were adorable.

The café was quiet and relatively orderly, so I decided to take the time to work on my neglected Thanksgiving menu. The holiday was going to be here before I knew it, and at this rate, I'd be serving my guests tiramisu and mozzarella-basil-tomato sandwiches from the café. Not exactly the traditional holiday feast I had in mind.

I grabbed a piece of paper and a pencil, dragged a stool up to the counter, and settled in to plan. I also wanted to figure out the timing as much as possible, so I found myself staring into space quite a bit as I did the mental calculations of how long things would take and what could be done simultaneously. Unfortunately, the angle I was sitting at meant that every time I looked up from my paper, I was looking right at Brent Griffin.

By the time I'd worked my way through the menu up to dessert, Mike came in. He'd apparently managed to get back home and put on real clothes since he was wearing his normal black suit. I secretly suspected he only had one.

"Hey, Fran. You ready to talk?"

"Sure thing. Let me just grab you a cup of coffee, and I'll be all set." I noticed Brent staring at me as I hopped down off my stool. "Is there anything I can get you, Brent?" I asked. I expected there wasn't, but I wanted to put him on the spot for staring.

He looked down at his computer without saying a word, and I headed triumphantly into the storage room. Of course, I had to come back for Mike's coffee as soon as I got in there and realized I'd forgotten it, but at least I had my moment.

"So what's up?" Mike asked after he'd downed the better half of the cup. I didn't know how he managed to drink such hot coffee so quickly.

I quickly told him the admittedly brief story about the security guards. "It's probably nothing, but you told me to let you know about anything remotely suspicious," I finished. I studied his face to see if I could read his expression. It was a very Mike expression—lips tight and brow furrowed in a look that either indicated he was deep in thought or very unhappy.

"You're right," he said when I was about to apologize for bothering him with my silly imagined problems. "It could be nothing. Anyone could have seen that window this morning before it got cleaned up, or even last night before Sammy found it." He frowned deeper. "Although I'd hope they would have called us if they had. In any case, it was very visible, and plenty of people saw it." He took a deep breath in and let it out slowly. "What bothers me is that he apparently made a point of mentioning it to you even after the window was cleaned off and"–he paused to whip his notebook out of his pocket and flip through its pages until he found what he was looking for–"that he used the same phrase about your knowledge of security that he used during your previous conversation. Is that accurate?"

I nodded. "It definitely felt like he was reminding me of that."

He tapped his pen on the notebook. "I think it's worth looking into. Hopefully, he was just being a jerk, but in case he wasn't, he and I should have a chat." He pulled out his phone and tapped at the screen a few times before holding it up to his ear. "Hey, it's Stanton. I need you to bring in the guys from Kandinsky who were working the museum the night of the robbery... No, just tell them I have some follow-up questions... Yeah... Uh-huh... Yeah, let me know when they're there... All right, talk to you later." He hung up and smiled at me. "I'll let you know what I find out."

I smiled back. "Thanks, Mike."

"Just doing my job." He paused. "And thank you for letting me do my job instead of running off and trying to do it yourself."

I held my hands up like I was surrendering. "Don't worry, I'm out. I'm done investigating crimes. From now on, I'm just making coffee."

"That's what I like to hear."

"Can I top you off before you go?"

Mike shook his cup in his hand then tipped it back and drained it. "I'll take a full cup if you don't mind."

I stared at him. "How do you sleep at night?"

He shrugged and grinned. "I cut myself off around eight or nine."

"And that works?"

"I'm tired, Fran. Between the kids and this job, I'd sleep for days without the coffee. In fact, come Thanksgiving, I think that's what I'm going to do."

"I thought you were going to hide out in the woods."

"I am. I'm going to find an empty deer stand out in the woods and take a good long nap. I'll show up for the food."

I chuckled as I led him out into the café to refill his to-go cup. "Well, bundle up."

"I will." He took a surprisingly restrained sip from the cup I handed him. "Good stuff. Thanks, Fran. And don't hesitate to call me if anything else comes up."

"Okay, thanks."

Brent had torn himself away from his novel long enough to stare at us for some reason. Perhaps our banal coffee talk was providing him with inspiration for a critical scene.

Mike nodded at him as he walked by on his way out the door. Brent quickly looked back at his computer. I would be grateful when the Cliffton show ended just because it would mean I didn't have to deal with Brent and his overinflated ego anymore.

Chapter Eighteen

Sammy's shift was nearing its end when the café door opened and John, the retired art professor I'd seen at the opening of Cliffton's show, came in, lugging a bigger suitcase than I thought a man his age should be trying to manage on his own.

"John, let me help you with that." I hurried around the counter to grab the suitcase from him.

"Oh, no, Francesca, you don't need to do that. I have it."

"Please, I'm happy to do it." Both of our hands were on the handle now, but he seemed reluctant to let go. To a man his age, it was probably unthinkable to let a woman carry her own luggage, let alone to let her carry yours. But I wasn't giving in.

Reluctantly, he let go. I was surprised by the heft of the bag, but since I knew he'd been in town for at least a few days, I figured it must have been packed pretty full.

"Where would you like to sit?" I asked.

He looked around then gestured to a table near the counter. "Right there will be fine. Thank you, Francesca."

"Not a problem." I put the suitcase down on the floor next to the table.

"Would you mind terribly putting it closer to the wall? I wouldn't want anyone to trip over it."

"Sure," I replied. "Would you like me to put it in the back room or behind the counter until you're ready to go? So it's out of the way?" It seemed like it would be a hassle to wedge the big suitcase behind the table only to drag it back out when he left.

He hesitated uncomfortably. "That's very kind of you, but the contents have quite a lot of sentimental value to me, and I'd rather keep them under close watch."

The customer is always right, so I pulled the table out, put the suitcase up against the wall, and then slid the table back into place. "How's that?"

"That'll be fine, thank you."

"So what can I get you? Let me guess, an americano."

"You have an excellent memory, Francesca," he said, smiling at me warmly.

"Is there anything else I can get you? A bite to eat maybe? It looks like you're heading out of town. You may as well fill up before you go."

"Do you have any more of that apple pie? The piece you served me the other day was delicious. I've been thinking about it ever since."

"Absolutely. Have a seat, and I'll bring it right over to you." I saw him reach for his wallet. "Put that away! I told you, I'm not charging a customer who's been coming here for sixty years."

"Well, there was a long gap between visits," he said, stepping over to the table and pulling out one of the chairs.

"Hopefully it won't be so long before we see you again." I smiled at him and went behind the counter to make his americano and grab a slice of the apple pie. When it was ready, I brought it around to his table.

"I don't suppose you want to sit down and have another chat?" he asked hopefully.

I glanced around the café to decide whether I could steal a few minutes to sit down with him. I noticed Sammy taking off her apron. "Actually, I have a better idea," I said. "I'll be right back." I hurried over to Sammy. "Hey!"

"Hey! What's up? Do you need me to stay a while longer? I can if you want me to," she offered in her typical pleasant Sammy fashion.

"Actually, I do, but not to work."

She raised her eyebrows.

"You have some time?"

She nodded.

"Come with me." I brought her over to John's table. "John, I have someone I want you to meet. This is Samantha Ericksen. Sammy, this is John, uh—" I looked at him to fill in his last name.

"Lewis," he said. "John Lewis. It's a pleasure to meet you, Samantha."

"Oh, call me Sammy," she said, shaking his hand.

"Not only is Sammy the one who keeps everything on track around here and makes sure I actually remember to put things like apple pie on the menu, she also happens to be a very talented artist," I said.

"Oh, Fran, stop," Sammy said modestly.

"No, really, she is. She does all the menu boards for the café, but–" I looked up at the boards, neatly written and decorated with line drawings of leaves and vines and pumpkins for fall. "Well, those don't really show off her talent." I turned to Sammy. "John, here, was an art professor up in Boston for fifty years before he retired."

Sammy's eyes lit up. "Really?"

"Really. Although, I assure you, it's not that impressive of a credential. Once you have tenure, you can stay until you retire or die. I did them the favor of choosing the former and not making them wait for the latter."

"Oh, stop. I'm sure they would have been thrilled to have you for another fifty years!" Sammy slid into the chair opposite John without hesitation. I was happy to see that my instinct that they would get along was on the mark.

I excused myself and headed back to the counter. The two of them were already chatting away. "You know, you remind me of a girlfriend I used to have, many, many years ago, before your parents were even born, I would wager. She had the same angelic look as you. She worked here too, back when it was new," I heard him say.

"Oh, thank you!" Sammy replied. "That's so kind."

Happy with myself, I set about preparing the day's pies.

A few hours, ten pies, and about a million cappuccinos, lattes, and americanos later, Rhonda and I finished cleaning up the café and locked it up for the night. After the morning's excitement, the rest of the day had proceeded uneventfully. I tried to convince her that I didn't need an escort home, but she wasn't having it.

"Are you crazy?" she asked. "Somebody threatened you, followed you, and vandalized your café. You are not walking home by yourself tonight."

"I'm a grown woman. I take kickboxing. I can take care of myself," I replied.

"Sure you can. Right up until someone comes after you with a gun, or a baseball bat, or a machete."

"A machete?"

She shrugged. "It could happen."

"In Cape Bay? We're not exactly known for our swaths of impassable jungle."

"It's better not to risk it. There's safety in numbers and large vehicles made of steel and... I don't know, more steel." She picked up her keys. "Come on, I'm parked out back," she said.

There was no use in arguing. She had years of practice dealing with two intractable teenage boys who had a fundamental opposition to wearing long pants in winter, eating anything that wasn't processed and packaged, or picking their socks and dirty underwear up off the floor. She wasn't going to back down.

"Fine." I picked up my bag and followed Rhonda out the back.

She wasn't kidding when she mentioned the large steel vehicle. "I thought you had a minivan," I said.

"I do. I conned Dan into taking the boys to lacrosse practice, and all their stuff's in the van, so I brought Dan's truck."

I wasn't sure that "truck" was the right word for it. "Second home" might have been more accurate. It was one of the biggest SUVs I'd ever seen.

"How do you get in this thing?" I asked, standing on the passenger side with the door open. Rhonda had already managed to somehow levitate into the driver's seat.

"Running board. Grab the handle and pull yourself up."

I was skeptical. I put my bag on the floorboard, which was roughly at waist height, grabbed the handle above the door, stepped on the running board, and swung myself up into the car. It was like climbing a poorly designed ladder where the rungs were too far apart. "How do you do that all the time?" I asked.

Rhonda shrugged. "Gets easier with practice."

Three minutes later—because Rhonda drove the monstrosity slowly and took corners at a snail's pace—we turned onto my street.

"Is that a coyote?" Rhonda asked, slowing down even more and leaning forward to better see the scruffy critter trotting down the street.

I squinted to try to make it out. I didn't think it was a coyote, but—"That's Latte!"

"Your Latte?"

"We don't have multiple dogs on the street named Latte, Rhonda."

She shrugged. "You never know." She slowed the massive vehicle down even further.

I rolled down my window. "Latte! Latte!"

His ears perked up immediately, and he turned towards us. Rhonda stopped the ocean liner Dan was apparently trying to pass off as a road-legal method of transportation.

"Latte!" I called again. He started trotting towards us. I popped open the door, and he jumped in like it was no higher than my bed.

"He didn't have any trouble with it," Rhonda said.

"Watch it," I said. "Christmas is coming. You wouldn't want to see your hours suddenly get cut back."

Rhonda laughed. "You wouldn't either if you knew what I'm getting you."

And with that, I remembered that I needed to figure out something nice to do for my employees for Christmas.

"How did you get out, buddy?" I asked Latte, ruffling his ears.

"Did you let him out this morning and forget?"

"No, and even if I had, Matt was going to let him out before he left for Boston. I can't believe he would accidentally leave him out like that though."

Rhonda pulled up on the street in front of my house, and Latte and I hopped out. Well, Latte hopped. I slowly lowered myself to the ground, stumbling at the end when it turned out that it was even more of a drop than I thought.

I thanked her and waved goodbye. I was halfway up the sidewalk to my house when I realized she was still sitting there. I turned around and waved again.

"I'm just making sure there's no murderer waiting inside for you!" she called through the open window.

I rolled my eyes and finished walking up to the door. I was still fishing my keys out of my purse when Latte nudged the door open with his nose and walked inside.

My heart stopped. Matt accidentally leaving Latte outside was out of character, but I could see how it could happen under the right circumstances. Matt leaving the front door not just unlocked but not even latched was unfathomable. "Latte!" I called, backing down the sidewalk. "Latte, come here, boy! Latte!"

"Fran?" Rhonda called from the car. "What's going on?"

"I don't know," I said. "Latte!" He finally came to the door, looking like nothing was out of the ordinary, like he always roamed the streets and opened doors that were supposed to be locked. "Come here, Latte!" As soon as he started towards me, I turned and ran back to Rhonda's car. This time it was easier to fling myself up into it.

"What happened?" Rhonda asked as Latte hopped in behind me.

My hands were shaking so hard I could barely get my phone out of my pocket to dial Mike. "The door was open."

She rolled up the windows and hit the lock button.

"You're calling to tell me that everything is fine, right?" Mike said through the phone by way of greeting.

"When I got home from the café, Latte was outside and the front door wasn't closed all the way," I blurted out.

He said something indistinguishable to someone other than me before speaking into the phone again. "Where are you?" By the sounds in the background, he was moving around.

"At home," I replied, feeling like I was stating the obvious.

"Are you in the house?" I yanked the phone away from my head. His voice had come through it so loud that Rhonda jumped and Latte turned his head.

"Geez, Mike! You're supposed to just talk to me through the phone, not yell loud enough that I can hear you without it!"

"Fran, are you in the house?" he asked again. His voice was quieter and more controlled this time, but no less intense.

"No, of course not. How crazy do you think I am?"

"I wonder sometimes," he muttered. There were some muffled sounds, at least one of which sounded like a piece of fabric rubbing across the phone microphone. He must have been getting dressed. Second time in one day that I'd unceremoniously dragged him out of his house. I was on a roll. "So if you're not in the house, where are you? Tell me you're not standing at the front door."

"No, I'm in Rhonda's... car. She insisted on driving me home."

"It's a good thing she did too. I'm on my way over. Are you okay getting off the phone, or do you need me to stay on with you?"

"You can get off the phone," I said. I figured he wanted to call in some backup. Besides, I had Rhonda there with me.

"All right. Stay in the car. Keep the doors locked. Do not under any circumstances get out of the car. If anyone approaches you on foot or in a car, tell Rhonda to gun it out of there and go straight to the police station, do you understand?"

"Yes." I'd been scared and known it wasn't right for the door to be open like that, but

Mike's reaction was almost scaring me more.

"Call me if anything happens. I want to know if so much as a light turns on across the street, okay?"

"Okay."

"I'll be there in ten minutes." He disconnected the call just as unceremoniously as he'd answered it.

I sat there for a few seconds, breathing and trying to calm my racing heart.

"So, he wanted to know if you were in the house, huh?" Rhonda asked.

Despite the situation, I laughed. "Yeah, apparently he thinks I'm a total moron."

"He's just worried about you."

"By the way, he said to stay in the car and if anyone approaches us, you're supposed to"–I wiggled my fingers in the quote gesture–"gun it out of here."

"Yes, ma'am." She shifted the car into reverse and began backing down the street.

"What are you doing? Do you see someone?"

"Nope, we can just see the house better from here." She stopped the car in front of Matt's house.

With a sickening feeling, I realized I hadn't heard from Matt since he left for Boston. It was entirely possible—likely even—that he'd gotten to Boston, run straight into a meeting, and hadn't had a minute to himself to text me since then. But what if he was inside the house? What if—?

I wouldn't let myself think that. I punched up Matt's number on my phone. If he answered, it meant he was safe. If he didn't—well, it didn't mean anything. He could be in a meeting, or in the bathroom, or—probably just a meeting or the bathroom, I told myself.

The phone rang. Once. Twice. Three times. Even though it meant nothing, my hands were shaking again, and my breathing was getting harder.

"Matt?" Rhonda whispered.

I nodded. She reached over and squeezed my hand.

Midway through the fourth ring, Matt answered.

"Hey, Franny! What's up?" he asked, like nothing was going on.

"Matty, you're okay!"

"Uh, yeah." He paused for a second. "Are you okay?"

"Yeah, I just hadn't heard from you and wanted to make sure. I'll let you get back to whatever you were doing. I'll call you in a little bit." I knew he would worry if I told him what was going on. Now that I knew he was okay, I just wanted to get him off the phone and fill him in later, when I knew what exactly I was filling him in on.

"Wait, Franny, what's going on?"

"Nothing. I mean, nothing for you to worry about. I mean–" I realized this was a good opportunity to rule out one possibility for what was going on. "Hey, you don't think you could have accidentally left Latte outside, do you?"

"What? No! Of course not! Why? Is that what's going on? Is Latte okay?"

"Yes, he's fine. He's right here." He licked my hand for good measure. "And you made sure the front door was closed when you left, right?"

"Closed and locked. Franny, what's going on?"

"Oh, it's nothing. Rhonda was just worried about making sure I was safe. Oh, speak of the devil, she wants to talk to me about something. I'll call you in a little bit. Love you! Bye!"

"Love you too," he replied, sounding confused. I disconnected the call before he could get any ideas about saying anything else.

I felt bad about being less than fully honest with him, but I rationalized it by telling myself that I would explain it all when I called him back. Besides, he would only worry if I did tell him. He'd probably run out of whatever meeting or dinner he was in and drive home, even if whatever was going on would be long since over by the time he made it back.

"Don't want him to worry?" Rhonda asked.

"It wouldn't do any good," I replied. "I'll explain it all later."

She nodded, and we fell into an anxious silence.

For what seemed more like an hour than ten minutes, but was actually only four by the clock on the dash, we sat and stared at my house. Every time the wind blew a tree branch and made it twitch in my peripheral vision, I jumped. Rhonda, thankfully, was much cooler.

"I'm watching the mirrors," she said when I asked about it. I was glad she was staying pulled together. I felt like I was falling apart.

As soon as the numbers on the clock changed to show that four minutes had passed, a black car turned onto the street behind us.

"Rhonda!" I whispered.

"I see it," she said. Her hand hovered over the gearshift.

The car's headlights went out, and my chest seized in fear. Then, for a split second, the whole car seemed to light up in red and blue lights, and I realized it was just Mike. I nearly broke down in tears. He pulled up right in front of us and cut his engine.

Down the street, two marked police cars turned the corner, pulling over and stopping a couple of houses away from mine. Another marked car turned onto the street behind us and pulled up on the opposite side of the road from us. I wondered who Mike had dragged out of their houses—there was usually only one officer on duty during Cape Bay's overnight shift.

Mike and the other officers climbed out of their cars and met up in the street in front of my house. They talked for a minute or two then started walking towards my house. Two of the officers split off and went around the back. I felt like shouting to offer them my keys so they didn't have to break the door down, but I didn't think that would be looked highly upon.

Mike and the officer with him walked up to my front door, still wide open from where Latte had run in and out earlier. They flanked the door with their guns and flashlights drawn, just like on TV.

"They really do that, huh?" Rhonda said.

"I guess so."

For several anxiety-inducing seconds, they stood there. I'd seen Mike with his gun on his hip more times than I could count, but seeing him with it out was a whole different thing. It was borderline terrifying thinking that he might be using it in the next few minutes, and in my house no less.

Mike nodded his head, and then he and the other officer entered the house—slowly, like they were hoping to sneak up on anyone that was in there. For a few long minutes, Rhonda and I watched as flashlights bobbed around the house, first downstairs then upstairs. My stomach clenched as the lights shone in my bedroom. For a split second, I wondered if I'd made my bed that morning or, worse, left a bra or underwear lying out. That would be beyond mortifying. And then I remembered why they were in there and realized that they could find much worse things than some of my lacy underthings.

The lights went on in my room then the room that had been my mother's, then gradually all the lights downstairs came on.

"Should we go in?" Rhonda asked after a couple minutes of the lights being on but no one coming out.

"I don't think Mike would be too happy about that," I replied. "He specifically said not to get out of the car under any circumstances."

Rhonda looked at me with a mixture of surprise and admiration on her face. "You're showing a lot of restraint. I'm impressed."

I didn't tell her that it wasn't just me wanting to obey orders. I was also afraid to know what they found.

After a few more minutes, Mike came out of the house and motioned for us to come over. I noticed he was back in what must have been his standard rushing-out-of-the-house-on-police-business outfit of track pants and his Cape Bay Police Department sweatshirt.

"You coming?" I asked Rhonda as I popped my door open.

"I think it would be wise."

I fell out of the SUV-on-steroids, and Latte jumped down gracefully after me. I took a deep breath, glanced over at Rhonda for reassurance, and then led our little group over to my house.

"Well," Mike said as we reached him. "The good news is that whoever was inside is long gone."

"So someone was definitely in there?" I asked, feeling more than a little nauseous.

Mike nodded. "At least briefly, yes. Fortunately, nothing was disturbed as far as we can tell. We'll need you to verify that though. You do need to find somewhere else to stay tonight. Maybe with Rhonda?" He looked at her questioningly.

She nodded. "That's what I tried to convince her to do in the first place, but you know how she is."

I shot her a dirty look. Mike nodded. I shot him a dirty look too. Rhonda gave me a big, cheesy, teasing grin.

"Why do I need to find somewhere else to stay tonight?" I asked, hoping to veer the conversation away from what I sensed was about to become the two of them commiserating over how stubborn and willful I could be.

"They pried open the back door to gain access. The doorframe's splintered. You'll need to replace at least that, but probably the whole door."

I took a deep breath. "But that was all they did? Everything's okay otherwise?"

"That's what we need you to check. Come with me."

Mike escorted Rhonda, Latte, and me around the house, checking every room and closet for anything missing or out of order. There was nothing. And fortunately, I'd put all my unmentionables away and left my bed in a relatively orderly state.

"Since all they seem to have done was break in and let the dog out, I think their intention was to scare you more than anything else," he said after we'd circled back around to the living room.

"They endangered the life of my dog just to scare me? Couldn't they have accomplished that by just breaking in the back door?"

"Which upsets you more, the door or the dog?" Mike asked.

"The dog."

That night, lying in the surprisingly comfortable bed in Rhonda's guest room with Latte curled up by my side, I felt a white-hot rage creep over me.

It was one thing to mess with my café—sure, it upset me that someone would vandalize the business my grandparents had built and handed down to two generations now, but the spray paint cleaned off, and the place was insured. My dog was a completely different thing. He was a living, breathing creature who had been by my side through the toughest few months of my life. That someone would have so little regard for his life and safety infuriated me.

The vandalism of the café made me back off. The endangering of my dog was going to make me double down. Whoever the culprit was had made a grave mistake. I was going to find him and make him pay.

Chapter Nineteen

Despite the fact that I should have been—and actually was—exhausted from my three hours of sleep the night before and five or so hours a few nights before that, I lay awake most of the night, my brain going through the case detail by detail. It frustrated me that I couldn't figure out who did it—who would steal the painting and come after me.

The security guards seemed like a good possibility. They knew all the security systems that were in place in the museum, and they had worked in lots of museums, so they could have contacts to use to get rid of the painting—if they weren't harvesting it for materials, of course.

The biggest thing that made me suspect them was that mean streak the older one seemed to have. I could see him vandalizing the café and breaking into my house as his way of punishing me for asking questions about the museum security.

But I thought Brent had a good motive too—stealing the painting would punish his boss and give him more than enough money to fund his writing career. He had approved the security systems, but only after he made them weaker than what Mike recommended. Maybe that wasn't because he didn't want to pay for them but because he wanted the painting to be easier to take. And he certainly had the resources to sell it off.

Would he try to threaten me though? That was what I didn't know. They were such overt acts of aggression, and Brent seemed so... attached to his laptop. I wasn't sure I could picture him tearing himself away from it long enough to wreak havoc in my life.

And there was Adam Shuster. I hadn't talked to him. With all the pie baking I'd been doing, I'd been stuck at the café most of the time. I'd barely had time to go out to Honey Ballard's to talk to her. Even without talking to him though, I knew he had the access he would have needed to take the painting, and the contacts to sell it. I didn't know why he would threaten me since I hadn't even spoken to him, but everything I knew about him pointed to the fact that he had the temperament to do it if he had cause.

At some point in the night, I realized that was the thing that bothered me the most— no one really had cause to hurt me. I wasn't close to solving the case. I didn't even have someone I was leaning towards being the culprit. There was virtually nothing gained by scaring me off the case.

Sometime around dawn, I finally drifted off. I didn't sleep well with Rhonda's house coming alive shortly thereafter as she got her boys up and ready for school. From all the noise and the number of times I heard "Mom!" yelled out, it was no wonder she liked spending so much time at the café. What I considered noisy at the café was nothing compared to the racket coming from downstairs as I tried to sleep.

After the boys left, I managed to get a solid nap in before Rhonda was tapping on my door.

"What?" I moaned from under the covers, feeling like I was back in high school with my mom waking me up.

"I just wanted to let you know that it's almost ten. You don't have to get up or anything, but I wanted to make sure you knew."

"Thanks," I groaned.

"Does Latte need to go out?"

Latte, who had been sleeping the sleep of the dead until that second, popped his head up and started scrambling over me. "Apparently." I dragged myself out of the bed and stumbled over towards the door. "Sorry," I said, opening it. "I had trouble sleeping."

"Sleep as long as you like. I'll take care of Latte."

"Thanks," I replied before practically hurling myself back onto the bed. I don't remember my head even touching the pillow before I was back asleep.

I woke back up after about an hour, feeling strangely clearheaded despite the miniscule amount of sleep I'd gotten. I knew what I had to do. I popped out of bed, got a quick shower, threw on some clothes, and headed down to the living room where

Rhonda and Latte were sitting on the couch watching the morning chat shows.

"They just made the most amazing-looking bacon brown-butter pasta," she said. "I'm going to make it for dinner tonight."

"Will the boys appreciate something like that?" I asked, thinking of all the times she'd mentioned that they were more interested in inhaling half a dozen hot dogs for dinner than sitting down and enjoying something that their mother took ages to cook.

"No, but I will," she said and smiled. The show ended. "I have to go to the grocery store, but do you want to go grab lunch first?"

I hadn't ever been out to lunch with Rhonda. I realized it was probably something I should take her up on, but I had promised Sammy a couple of hours off so she could meet up for lunch with a friend who was passing through. "Next time," I told Rhonda.

"Oh, you're planning to have your house broken into and so have to spend the night here again sometime?"

"No, I mean, the next time you suggest it. As long as I don't have to be at the café or anything."

"I'm going to hold you to that, you know," Rhonda said.

"Trust me, I know."

On her way to the store, Rhonda ran me by Matt's house to drop off Latte and my overnight bag. I didn't want to leave Latte home all day in a strange house, and I didn't think Rhonda was too keen on the idea either, so Matt's house seemed like a safe alternative to her non-dog-proofed house and my broken-in one. Mike had nailed some boards across my back door the night before to keep it closed, but he wasn't sure that whoever broke in wasn't going to come back, and I wasn't about to risk Latte being let out again. When I talked to Matt, he said that it was more than okay to let Latte hang out at his place until he got home.

I'd finally called him to explain what was going on after I got to Rhonda's the night before. As I'd predicted, he got upset and wanted to come straight back to Cape Bay to be with me. After multiple assurances from both Rhonda and me that I was safely tucked away at her house, he finally agreed to stay up in Boston to finish his meetings. He'd be home sometime around dinnertime. I couldn't wait. I wanted nothing more than to be wrapped in his arms and know that I was safe.

But that would have to wait. Rhonda dropped me off at the café just in time for Sammy to leave for her lunch. The way I figured it, she'd be back right about the time Becky came in for her after-school shift. Between the two of them, I hoped that they would be able to cover the afternoon rush of high school kids, because that was the time I wanted to use to sneak away and go over to the museum to talk to Adam. There was still something that didn't fit together about the case, and he was the one person I hadn't talked to. I wasn't sure, but I felt like he might be the missing link.

Of course, it didn't work out quite that way. Sammy's lunch ran long, and Becky came in before she did. That wasn't really a problem except that with Becky came the rest of the high school crew, and I got caught up in filling their excessively complex drink orders. It seemed like they thought the longer it took them to place the order, the more mature it made them. No matter how hard I tried to convince them to just order a simple latte or americano, they always went for the five-part drink order. They were as bad as Brent Griffin and his nonfat soy mocha latte with extra whipped cream, but somehow they actually annoyed me less. Brent just brought out the worst in me. And of course he was there in the café too. I'd never quite been able to catch him, but I kept thinking I saw him staring at me while I'd been finalizing my Thanksgiving shopping list before the after-school rush.

Sammy finally got back just as the rush died down. She was apologetic but looked like she'd had a great time. When she was happy like that, she practically glowed. She really did look angelic like John Lewis had said the day before. Once she got her apron on and got settled in, I didn't have much time to make it to the museum, but it wasn't far, so I thought I could still manage it before she had to leave for the day. Becky, as good of a worker as she was, was a little too airheaded for me to trust in the café alone, especially after everything that had been going on.

I let Sammy know my plan and went in the back to grab my jacket and purse. I had almost made it out when I heard Becky say something that stopped me. She was talking to Sammy about the art class she was taking at school.

"—and today we talked about that Lewis Cliffton guy who has his art show in town," she said.

"Oh, it's pronounced Louie," Sammy said, correcting her gently.

"Really?" Becky asked, squinching up her nose. "Are you sure?"

"Pretty sure. Fran?"

"Yup, it's loo-ee," I replied. Something about it was tickling my brain.

"But it's spelled like it should be Lewis," Becky said.

"It's the French pronunciation," Sammy said.

"Why would you spell your kid's name like that though? If you want him to be called Louie, why not name him Louie?"

Sammy shrugged. "It's not uncommon." She glanced over at me, looking for backup from the barrage of teenage borderline logical reasoning, but I was trying to figure out what it was about what Becky said that felt important.

"I mean, your kid is going to be called Lewis at least once in a while if you spell his name L-o-u-i-s, right? I can't be the only one who thinks that doesn't make sense."

"Maybe it's a family name," Sammy said.

In an instant, everything clicked into place. "Sammy, I'm going to take longer than I planned. I'll call you and explain in a little bit. And can you call Rhonda to come in and cover for me?" I was out the door without even waiting for her reply. I had to go to Boston.

Chapter Twenty

Two hours later—because of traffic and the terrible Boston drivers—I pulled up in front of the house on Beacon Street that Sammy had texted me the address of after I called her in the car on the way up. My hands were shaking. If I was wrong, I would be beyond embarrassed. But I knew I wasn't wrong. Deep down, I knew.

I walked up the steps to the door and, after a moment's hesitation and a few deep breaths, rang the bell. I was about to ring it again when the door opened.

"Francesca! What a pleasant surprise. Please come in. What brings you all the way up here?"

The warm greeting made me doubt what I was about to do, but there was no turning back now. I stepped inside, and he closed the door behind me. I stared at him mutely for a few seconds, trying to make my dry mouth work.

"Francesca, are you all right?"

"John, where's the painting?"

My heart nearly broke as the old man's face fell. "Come with me," he said and led me up the stairs and down the hall to the back of the house. He opened the door to his bedroom. At any other time, I would have been awed by the view of the Charles River, but under the circumstances, I barely noticed it. He crossed the room and gestured to an alcove by the bed.

There it was. Cliffton's painting. In the homey apartment, it was even more beautiful than I'd remembered it from the sterile museum. The way the light from the windows caught it, the tear trickling down Cliffton's mother's face was unmistakable.

"Elizabeth and I were in art school together," John said quietly. "She was so talented. She could have been the next Mary Cassatt or Berthe Morisot. In the summers, she'd go back home to Cape Bay and work in the café to make money to pay for art supplies. I couldn't stand to be away from her for so long, so I'd drive down to see her. Her parents wanted better for her than to marry an artist, so we had to sneak around. I'd drive down in the morning and spend the day in the café, just watching her work. We'd sneak away to the beach during her breaks to be alone together. Your grandfather—he gave her a lot of breaks on those days."

"My grandfather was a great believer in true love."

He smiled faintly and closed his eyes, taking a deep, ragged breath. "When she became pregnant, I wanted to marry her. We'd have been poor, but we would have been happy. But her parents wouldn't allow it. They said they'd disown her if she married me. They told her we'd be poor and that the baby would starve to death for want of food. They said she would spend her days working her fingers to the bone working for other people just to keep the baby alive. That she'd never touch a paintbrush again. They assailed her night and day with all the horrible things that would happen if she married me. In the end, I think she just couldn't take it anymore. She met me one night on the beach and told me she couldn't see me anymore. I begged, I pleaded with her to run away with me. I told her we didn't need her family, that our little family would be happy on our own. Then she told me that she'd lost the baby. The stress had been too much for her, and she'd lost it. She said she didn't love me anymore. She never wanted to see me again. I remember falling to the sand and weeping until my tears ran dry."

He stopped, clearly lost in the memory of that night so many years ago. After a moment, he gathered himself and continued. "The next day, she married Edward Cliffton. He was a society boy whose family summered in Cape Bay. His parents were less than pleased with him marrying a local girl like her, but her parents could not have been happier. He was exactly what they wanted for her. Exactly the opposite of me."

"Did you ever see her again?"

"Only on the society pages. But seven months later, I received this." He opened a drawer in the nightstand, pulled out a yellowed card, and handed it to me.

It was a birth announcement. For Louis John Cliffton. In the corner a message was written in delicate handwriting. "I'm sorry I lied. I will always love you.–E."

"I have no idea of how she convinced him of that name. I suppose he never knew mine. He probably never bothered to ask."

"What about her parents?" I asked hoarsely.

"They died in a car accident six months after she married him. They never knew the baby."

The tears streamed openly down my face as I handed the birth announcement back to him. It was the saddest story I'd ever heard. "But why did you take the painting?" I asked. I understood why he felt connected to it, but not why he'd stolen it.

"I'm dying, Francesca. Pancreatic cancer. The doctors say I have just a few months to live. I didn't go to the show with the intention of stealing anything, but when I saw it, I felt as though Elizabeth were there with me again. I was alone in the gallery at the end of the evening, and I thought, this is my chance to be with Elizabeth again just for a little while. I took it off the wall and walked out the back door. I was certain they would find me. I waited in that hotel for days, dreaming of her and our days on the beach. When no one came, I thought it must have been a sign from Elizabeth that I was supposed to bring her back here to the home we would have shared. I'll be dead soon. They'll find the painting then and return it to Louis. It's like I'm just borrowing it for a time." He studied my tear-streaked face. "Are you going to turn me in, Francesca?"

I didn't know. I think I could bring myself to do it, but keeping the secret would be a crime in and of itself. It would only be for a matter of months, but if someone else was able to figure it out just like I had—I sighed. I didn't want to make this decision. And then I remembered that my house had been broken into and my café had been vandalized—my life had been threatened. I couldn't quite bring myself to be angry with the broken old man beside me, but I didn't understand why he would have done those things either. I hadn't had the slightest inkling that he was involved until Becky had commented about Cliffton's name.

"I don't know yet," I said. "First, tell me this—why did you threaten me? Why did you follow me and vandalize Antonia's and break into my house? Why did you leave my dog out to roam the streets?"

"What do you mean? I didn't do any of those things, Francesca. I would never harm or threaten to harm someone. I'm a peaceful man." The look on his face told me he wasn't lying. He had no idea what I was talking about.

Someone else—for some reason—had been trying to scare me off investigating the case. It was an even more terrifying prospect than that of the art thief harassing me—someone was doing it, and I didn't know why.

"I'm—I'm sorry," I stammered. "I just thought—I thought the two were connected. The missing painting and the threats. I shouldn't have accused you. I, um—" My head was reeling. I could barely put a thought together.

"I think you need to sit down. Come downstairs, and join me in the sitting room. I wouldn't dare offer you a cup of coffee, but do you drink tea? A nice cup of tea may be just what you need."

He led me downstairs and sat me on the couch while he prepared the tea. As we sat and sipped it, I asked more questions about his life. I was saddened to hear that he had given up painting after he and Elizabeth broke up and that he'd never had so much as a sweetheart again. He'd been an only child and quite literally had no one left in the world.

Except Cliffton. The thought stuck with me through the rest of our conversation right up until he walked me to the door.

"Does Louis know he's your son?" I asked.

"I don't believe so, no."

"You should tell him."

"I don't think I could do that. His mother has just died. He doesn't need to find out about me only to have me die in a few months' time."

"You should at least tell him that you knew his mother then. I didn't talk to him long, but it was obvious how much he loved her."

"Perhaps I'll do that. It would be nice to talk about her."

I gave him a hug goodbye and promised to come see him again. I descended the stairs, got into my car, waved goodbye, and drove away. I only hoped I'd make it back before he died.

I called Matt on my way back to Cape Bay to let him know that he might beat me back. I offered to pick up some takeout on my way back, but he said he wanted to cook for me. I agreed, even though that meant that I wouldn't make up any ground in our who-pays-for-dinner competition. He was leading by an embarrassingly large margin.

"Spaghetti or polenta?" I asked him. They were the only two things he knew how to cook, and the polenta was something he'd only just learned when we took a cooking class while we were in Italy.

Before he could answer, my phone beeped to tell me I had another call coming in. I looked at the information my phone was beaming to my dashboard. Mike. I told Matt I'd call him back and switched over to Mike's call.

"Hi, Mike!"

"Where are you?" he barked.

"What? In my car. Near Plymouth. Why?"

"Oh, thank God."

"What? Why? What's going on?" An icy blade of fear that something had happened to one of the girls at the café stabbed my heart.

"One of your neighbors saw some suspicious movement in your house and called us. We arrested Brent Griffin in your bedroom five minutes ago."

Chapter Twenty-One

The doorbell rang.

"Want me to get it?" Matt asked.

"No, I got it," I replied.

"Are you sure?" He glanced at my flour-covered hands.

"Yup." I brushed them off on my red, white, and green *Italia!*-emblazoned apron. "See?" I kissed him and went to answer the door.

"Happy Thanksgiving!" Mike said as he shoved a bottle of wine at me as soon as I opened the door.

"Well, hello to you too!" I replied.

He looked me over. "Kind of dressed for the wrong holiday there, aren't you?"

I gestured at the *Italia!* across my chest. "It's never the wrong holiday to be proud of your heritage, Mike. Do you want to come in?"

He looked down at his wristwatch. "Yeah, I can spare a couple of minutes."

"Are you headed up to your in-laws' cabin in the mountains?"

"Yup. And as long as I make it by dinner at three, Sandra will be fine."

I led Mike into the kitchen.

"Let's go Pats!" he said when he laid eyes on Matt in his full New England Patriots regalia.

"Let's go Pats!" Matt replied.

"Can I get you anything to eat or drink?" I asked, hoping to cut off the ritual football blather before it went any further. "I have cinnamon rolls, pumpkin spice muffins, coffee of course."

"You don't have to-go cups, do you?" Mike asked.

"No, but I have regular ones you can borrow." I started the coffee machine up and went to get my biggest travel mug for Mike. I didn't need to wait for him to actually say that's what he wanted. That's what Mike always wanted.

"Thanks, Franny, you're the best." Mike pulled up a chair at the table and helped himself to one of the fresh cinnamon rolls sitting on it.

"So, do you have any news?" Matt asked, saying what I was thinking. I was glad I didn't have to bring it up.

"Yes, I do," Mike said around a bite of cinnamon roll. I waited impatiently for him to finish chewing. "Brent Griffin pleaded guilty yesterday afternoon to three counts of embezzlement, one count of vandalism, and two counts of burglary."

I exhaled a sigh of relief.

"That was fast," Matt said.

"Yup. He insisted on pleading out immediately, against his lawyer's advice."

"He's going to jail, right?" I asked, depositing Mike's coffee on the table.

He laughed. "Oh, yeah. For a long time too. He took the first deal the prosecutor offered."

"He probably thinks jail will give him more time to work on his novel."

Mike choked on a big swig of his coffee.

"What?" I asked.

Mike's mouth twitched like he was barely containing himself. "He did mention that in front of the judge."

"Are you serious?"

"As serious as a prison sentence for embezzlement. You should have seen the look on the judge's face when he said that."

I tried to picture smug Brent standing in front of the judge saying that he was looking forward to spending his prison sentence working on his novel. I could actually see it. And I wouldn't have been surprised if he started trying to give the judge a summary of the character arcs either.

I still couldn't believe the way it had all played out. Mike had filled me in after I got home from Boston the night Brent was arrested. He hadn't stolen the painting to get the money to fund his writing—he hadn't needed it.

He'd been stealing money from Cliffton for years. Hundreds of thousands of dollars taken from under the artist's nose. Under-recording a sale here, overrecording a payment there. He'd been slowly but surely socking it away the entire time he'd worked for Cliffton.

And that's what had happened with the lax security system at the museum that had led to the painting being stolen. Brent had written a check out of Cliffton's account for the full amount of Mike's quoted system but cashed it himself and only turned over the money for a fraction of what was really needed, pocketing the rest. It was my questions about the security system and Brent's handling of Cliffton's finances that led him to think that I was on to him. Apparently, that's what Brent thought I was talking to Mike about.

I realized in retrospect that the times I'd thought he was staring at me while I worked on my Thanksgiving menu, he actually thought I was making notes about my findings to turn over to Mike. That was why he'd started threatening me—to get me to lay off the case. And when he saw me take off out of the café the day I'd gone to Boston, he thought I was going to give Mike some mythical last bit of evidence. We'd never quite figured out whether he'd been in my bedroom looking for my notes about the case—which, of course, didn't exist—or for something else, but I really didn't want to know either way. I was just glad it was over.

"You know, I actually feel kind of bad for him," I said.

Matt and Mike both looked at me like I'd lost my mind.

"No, really. He created this whole conspiracy out of nowhere. It was all in his head. None of it was real. And now he's in jail because of it. If he hadn't decided that I was on to him, it could have been years before his embezzling came out. He'd even told me that he was planning on quitting his job with Cliffton. If he had, he might even have gotten away scot-free. He was a victim of his own imagination."

For a second, it seemed like they both found my thoughts insightful. And then Mike spoke up.

"No, Fran. It's much less poetic than that. He was a victim of his own arrogance, like most of them are. Everybody thinks they're so smart that they'll get away with it, but most of the time it's just dumb luck when they do." He pushed the last of the cinnamon bun in his mouth and washed it down with what I estimated to be the better part of the cup of coffee. I went ahead and started the coffee machine to refill his cup.

"I guess you're right," I said.

"Yes, I am," he replied.

I refilled his astoundingly empty coffee cup and handed it back to him.

"I'd better get going. Mind if I take one for the road?" he asked, picking up another cinnamon bun.

"Not at all. Let me get you something to wrap it in."

"It's not going to last long enough for you to worry about it." He stood up and raised the coffee cup in a toast. "Happy Thanksgiving, you two. And let's go Pats!"

"Let's go Pats!" Matt echoed immediately. I worked on shooing Mike towards the door.

Just outside, he turned and looked back at me. "So you're still not going to tell me what you were doing up in Boston that day, huh?"

I shook my head. "Nope. Like I said, it was touchy-feely girlie emotional stuff. You wouldn't be interested."

"You know, I doubt that." He tipped his cup towards me again. "Happy Thanksgiving, Fran. And please try to stay out of my cases from now on."

I couldn't help but grin. "Trust me," I said. "After this, I want nothing to do with any of them ever again."

"I feel like I've heard that before." He turned away from me and headed down the front walk.

"Drive safe!" I called. "Tell Sandra and the kids I said hello!"

"Will do!"

I watched him drive away and then went back inside.

"It's funny how the art theft case just went away," Matt said as I wrapped my arms around him from behind. "It was international news and then just, nope, never mind."

"It sounded like it was just a big misunderstanding."

"You really believe that, Franny?"

"I do."

"Really? Cliffton just happened to find his long-lost biological father right before the show, promised him the painting of his mother, and then forgot all about it for two weeks while the Cape Bay PD and Massachusetts State Police and FBI searched for the stolen painting? You believe that?"

"Sure do."

"And this long-lost father who's dying but seems like he's in perfectly good mental shape just completely misunderstood that he wasn't supposed to take the painting off the wall of the museum and carry it home with him instead of leaving it until the end of the exhibition? You believe that too?"

"Yup."

"And he never thought to come forward when it was all over the news that the painting was stolen."

"Sounds plausible."

Matt rotated in my arms so he could put his around me too. "Francesca Amaro, you really believe all that?"

I nodded my head against his chest. He put one finger under my chin and tipped it up towards him. A smile played at his lips. "What were you doing in Boston that day?"

"Have I ever told you the most heart-breaking and beautiful love story I've ever heard?"

"Is it ours?"

I swatted my hand against his back. "Ours better not be heartbreaking!" I laughed.

"Oh, then no. Tell me."

"It all started in Cape Bay, over sixty years ago now—"

Before I could get any further, the doorbell rang.

"Oh, that'll be Ryan and Sammy!" I said, pulling away from Matt. "I'll have to tell it to you some other time."

I knew that Matt and Mike both suspected I had something to do with the sudden turn in the art theft case, but neither of them knew quite what.

One day, maybe in a few months, when it didn't matter anymore, I might tell them. But for now, it wasn't my story to tell.

Recipe 1: Apple Pie

Ingredients:
- 6 cups apples, thinly sliced
- 3/4 cup sugar
- 1 tbsp butter
- 1 tsp ground cinnamon

Pie Crust:
- 3 cups all-purpose flour
- 3/4 cup vegetable oil
- 1/3 cup milk
- 1 tsp salt

Preheat over for 425F.

For pie crust, sift flour twice, then whisk in salt. Pour in oil, followed by milk and stir. Finish dough by gently kneading it on wax paper. Divide into two pieces. Roll out dough and line pie plate with one. If short on time, store-bought pie crust will do.

Core, peel and slice apples. Combine sugar and cinnamon in a bowl. Arrange layers of apples on lined pie plate, sprinkling each layer with sugar and cinnamon. Dot top layer with small pieces of butter. Cover top with crust. If not using lattice strips, make sure to cut out for air ventilation while baking. It would be cute to use a cookie cutter. Press edges of crust together.

Bake for 20-25 minutes, or until the crust is golden brown. Let cool before serving.

Recipe 2: Americano

Ingredients:
- Espresso
- Hot water

Use an espresso maker to make an espresso shot. Pour into a glass or mug. Pour an equal amount of hot water into it. If you prefer something milder, double the amount of water per shot (2:1).

About the Author

Harper Lin is the USA TODAY bestselling author of *The Patisserie Mysteries*, *The Emma Wild Holiday Mysteries*, *The Wonder Cats Mysteries*, and *The Cape Bay Cafe Mysteries*.

When she's not reading or writing mysteries, she loves going to yoga classes, hiking, and hanging out with her family and friends.

www.HarperLin.com

Harper Lin